Legend of Burning Water

DEDICATION

*With love to Gerda,
my mother*

*The home you provided
gave all of us courage
to journey*

To Briana, with my love. "goodie"

LEGEND
OF BURNING
WATER

SIGMUND BROUWER

VICTOR BOOKS

A DIVISION OF SCRIPTURE PRESS PUBLICATIONS INC.
USA CANADA ENGLAND

Easter - 1994.

THE WINDS OF LIGHT SERIES
Wings of an Angel
Barbarians from the Isle
Legend of Burning Water
The Forsaken Crusade

Cover design by Mardelle Ayres
Cover illustration by Jeff Haynie
Photo by Dwight Arthur

Library of Congress Cataloging-in-Publication Data:

Brouwer, Sigmund, 1959–
    Legend of burning water / by Sigmund Brouwer.
      p.   cm. — (Winds of light series : #3)
    Summary: In 1313, Thomas risks his life to gain possession of an English manor that was stolen from its rightful owners.
    ISBN 0-89693-115-3
    [1. Knights and knighthood — Fiction. 2. Civilization, Medieval — Fiction. 3. England — Fiction. 4. Christian life — Fiction.]
    I. Title. II. Series.
    PZ7.B79984Wi   1992
    [Fic] — dc20
                                               91-38487
                                                CIP
                                                    AC

1 2 3 4 5 6 7 8 9 10 Printing/Year 96 95 94 93 92

VICTOR BOOKS
A division of SP Publications, Inc.
Wheaton, Illinois 60187

AUTHOR'S NOTE

For two thousand years—far north and east of London—the ancient English towns of Pickering, Thirsk, and Helmsley, and their castles, have guarded a line on the lowland plains between the larger centers of Scarborough and York.

In the beginning, Scarborough, with its high North Sea cliffs, was a Roman signal post. From there, sentries could easily see approaching barbarian ships, and were able to relay messages from Pickering to Helmsley to Thirsk, the entire fifty miles inland to the boundary outpost of York, where other troops waited—always ready—for any inland invasions.

When their empire fell, the Romans in England succumbed to the Anglo-Saxons, great savage brutes in tribal units who conquered as warriors, and over the generations became farmers. The Anglo-Saxons in turn suffered defeat by raiding Vikings, who in turn lost to the Norman knights from France with their thundering war-horses.

Through those hundreds and hundreds of years, that line from Scarborough to York never diminished in importance.

Some of England's greatest and richest abbeys—religious retreats for monks—accumulated their wealth on the lowland plains along that line. Rievaulx Abbey, just outside Helmsley, contained 250 monks and owned vast estates of land which held over 13,000 sheep.

But directly north, lay the moors.

No towns or abbeys tamed the moors, which reached east hundreds of square miles to the craggy cliffs of the cold gray North Sea.

Each treeless and windswept moor plunged into deep dividing valleys of lush greenness that only made the heather-covered heights appear more harsh. The ancients called these North York moors "Blackamoor".

Thus, in the medieval age of chivalry, 250 years after the Norman knights had toppled the English throne, this remoteness and isolation protected Blackamoor's earldom of Magnus from the prying eyes of King Edward II and the rest of his royal court in London.

Magnus, as a kingdom within a kingdom, was small in comparison to the properties of England's greater earls. This smallness too was protection. Hard to reach and easy to defend, British and Scottish kings chose to overlook it, and in practical terms, it had as much independence as a separate country.

Magnus still had size, however. Its castle commanded and protected a large village and many vast moors. Each valley between the moors averaged a full day's travel by foot. Atop the moors, great flocks of sheep grazed on the tender green shoots of heather. The valley interiors supported cattle and cultivated plots of land, farmed by peasants nearly made slaves by the yearly tribute exacted from their crops. In short, with sheep and wool and cattle and land, Magnus was not a poor earldom, and well worth ruling.

The entire story of Magnus is difficult to relate in a single

volume. *The Legend of Burning Water* follows two portions of its
tale which relate how the orphan boy Thomas—then 14 and in
those times old enough to be considered a man—conquered
Magnus and released its village from murderous oppression.
(That part of the tale is told in *Wings of an Angel.*)

Yet, along with power, a lordship has its responsibilities.
Thomas must protect his people, and the second volume of the
story of Magnus (*Barbarians from the Isle*) tells how Thomas bat-
tled the powerful northern Scots, then faced a far greater trial,
one imposed by Druid false sorcerers who demanded he join
their secret group, or lose his lordship and castle.

As this volume begins, Thomas almost feels secure within his
kingdom. Three seasons have passed—without incident—since
Thomas narrowly defeated that bid by false sorcerers to reconquer Magnus. Yet he dreads the return of the Druids.

Those interested in ancient times should know that Magnus
itself cannot be found in any history book. Nor can Thomas be
found. Nor his nurse Sarah, the wandering knight Sir William,
Katherine, Geoffrey the Candlemaker, Tiny John, nor others of
the collection of friends and foes of Thomas. Yet many of the
more famous people and events found throughout its story
shaped the times of that world, as historians may easily confirm.

KATHERINE
The Departure
MIDSUMMER A. D. 1312

They looked down from the edge of a slight crest, an old man and a girl (almost woman). Behind them, on the flat of the crest, a small fire smoldered to its gray death beside two blankets rolled into tight bundles. On the other side of the fire stood a small brown mule, its front legs hobbled by a slack piece of rope. Further back of the mule, the hill rose steeply away from the crest to final heights of windswept heather.

The girl shivered away the last of her sleepiness against the dawn's cold. The old man's cloak and hood wrapped him in a darkness which almost concealed the cane that supported him as he leaned forward to survey the castle below.

Music reached them faintly.

"This celebration promises to rival that of the day when Thomas first freed the kingdom," the old man remarked. "Their song and dance has carried them the night through, and not even the first light of morning sends the people of Magnus to their beds."

Katherine, the girl stared downward at the tiny pieces of

color which were festive flags lined along the top of the castle walls far below.

"Must such pain always come with duty?" she asked quietly. "The years I spent disguised as a pitiful freak are nothing compared to the ache I feel now to depart from Magnus as I did."

"Would you wish to return?" the old man asked in reply.

"Only to tell Thomas the truth." She did not add to her statement another thought, *and to have him hold me again.*

The flat gray sky brightened to its first tinge of blue before the old man spoke again. "Until we are certain of which side he chooses, he cannot know of us. Or of his destiny."

"You have said that oft before!" Katherine's quick words betrayed more than a trace of impatience. She swept her hands to indicate the castle below. "Yet all of Magnus is in celebration because yesterday Thomas survived trial by ordeal, a trial he withstood because he refused to belong to the Druid circle of evil. Is that not enough proof of choice?"

"Is it indeed?"

The calmness of his statement caused her to falter. "Is it not?" Katherine almost pleaded.

The old man sighed. "We play against unseen masters a terrible and mysterious game of chess, Katherine. As you well know, Thomas belonged to us at birth. Too soon, we had no choice but to leave him among them, alone and only armed with those few books of knowledge. But many years have passed. We do not know if they have claimed him as their own."

"Thomas conquered Magnus," Katherine protested. "Even without knowing the true purpose of that destiny. He rejected their offer of unlimited wealth and power—I stood in the secret passageway and heard clearly every word. Surely that is enough proof he is not one of them."

The old man shifted his weight. Again, the sky grew deeper in blue before he answered. A light breeze began to move along the slope of the valley hills, and pulled wisps of Katherine's long blond hair forward against her face.

"In this terrible game of chess, nothing is what it appears to be," the old man said. "How can we know they have not artfully arranged a simple deception? After all, the more it would seem Thomas is not one of them, the more likely we might finally tell him the truth. To do so—should Thomas be one of them—is to arm them with what they so desperately seek. The consequence? Centuries of battle lost in the quickest of heartbeats."

"If he not be one of them? But, rather, one of us?" Katherine persisted. "His victory yesterday will only make them more determined. Yet how is Thomas to survive if he knows not what he fights?"

Passion filled her cheeks with color. "And has he not done enough already? He has defeated the Druid attempt at rebellion within Magnus. He has turned away the most powerful earl in the north," Katherine said. "Yet the Druids have not been completely conquered. As well, the Earl of York has departed as a sworn enemy—a mystery which bewilders and torments Thomas. He and Magnus are not free from danger!"

"You were not the only spy in Magnus," the old man said softly without removing his gaze from the castle below. "Thomas shall be watched. And guided. His death—should it occur—will be sad proof that he was not capable of carrying on our battle."

The old man straightened and slowly turned to the fire and the mule. He pretended not to see the grief which spasmed across Katherine's face. She was 15, nearly woman, but far too young for such pain.

"We have waited too long already," he said. "Magnus is no longer safe for us. Our own journey must begin."

THOMAS
Exiled

SPRING A. D. 1313

Each day, the guards on the castle walls expected Tiny John to appear shortly after *terce*, the ringing of the bells which marked the 9 A.M. devotional services. By then, Tiny John would already have visited half the shopkeepers' stalls in Magnus.

The guards had good reason to watch for him; few were they who had not been plucked of loose coins by the rascal pickpocket. A temporary loss of silver—because Tiny John would return it without fail the next day—meant nothing. It was the ribbing of other guards which always left the victim red-faced and huffing with indignation. After all, how could any military man keep self-respect if robbed by an eight-year-old?

None, however, were the guards who could carry a grudge against Tiny John. He had been in Magnus since the previous summer, yet that lopsided grin which flashed from his smudged face was welcomed like the bright colors of a cheerful bird in every corner of the village, especially throughout an exhausting and long winter.

And, even without the charm of a born rascal, Tiny John was

always safe within Magnus. The lord Thomas, who ruled with unquestioned authority, considered him a special—if untamable—friend.

Before the bells of *terce* stopped echoing this spring morning, Tiny John had already scampered from the first castle wall turret to the next. He dodged the two gruff guards between like a puppy whirling with glee among clumsy cattle.

" 'Tis a fine kettle of fish, soldier Alfred!" Tiny John shouted through his grin at the second guard. "All the tongues in town waggle about the sly looks you earn from tanner's daughter. And with her betrothed to a mason at that!"

Tiny John waited, hunched over with his hands on his knees, ready for flight after the delivered insult.

"Let me get a grasp 'a you," soldier Alfred grunted as he lunged at Tiny John, "then we'll see how eager you might be to discuss these matters."

Tiny John laughed, then ducked to his right. And made a rare mistake. He misjudged the slipperiness of the wet stone below his feet, and fell flat backward.

"Ho! Ho!" A moment later, soldier Alfred scooped him into burly arms, grabbed him by the scruff of his shirt and the back of his pants and hoisted him halfway over the castle walls.

"Scoundrel," Alfred laughed, "tell me what you see below."

"Water," Tiny John gasped. A weak spring sun glinted gray off the waves of the small lake which surrounded the castle island.

"Water indeed. Perhaps for a fine kettle of fish?"

"Wonderful jest," Tiny John managed to say upward to his captor. The fall had winded him, and it was still difficult for his lungs to find air. "T'is easy to understand why the tanner's daughter would be taken with such a man as yourself."

"Aaargh!" Alfred grunted. "What's to be done with you?"

"A reward perhaps?" Tiny John asked.

Alfred set him back down on his feet and dusted off the small boy's back.

"Reward indeed. Be on your way."

"I speak truth," Tiny John protested. "Because of me, you shall be the first to sound alarm."

"Eh?" Alfred squinted as he followed Tiny John's pointing arm to look beyond the lake.

"There," Tiny John said firmly, "from the trees at the edge of the valley. A progression of fifteen men. None on horseback."

It took several minutes for Alfred to detect the faraway movement. Then he shouted for a messenger to reach the Sheriff of Magnus.

Moments later, Alfred shouted again. This time in disgust. His now-empty pouch no longer carried any farthings.

Tiny John, of course, had disappeared.

Rich, thick tapestries covered each wall of the royal chamber. Low benches lined each side, designed to give peasants with appeals rest as they waited each morning for decisions from their lord on his throne.

At the back of that chamber, Thomas leaned casually against the large ornate chair which served as his throne. He waited for the huge double doors at the front to close behind his entering sheriff, Robert of Uleran.

Thomas' last glimpse beyond, as usual, was of the four guards posted out front, each armed with long pike and short sword. And, as usual, it irritated him to be reminded that double guard duty remained necessary.

"The arrival of fifteen men?" Thomas asked to break their solitary silence.

"Exactly as Alfred spoke," Robert of Uleran replied to his lord.

"Although I confess surprise at his accuracy, and the earliness of his warning. He is not known for sharp eyes."

Thomas smiled in agreement and pulled one of the long padded benches away from the wall and sat down. With a motion of his hand, he invited Robert of Uleran to do the same.

"Have the visitors been thoroughly searched?" Thomas asked.

Robert of Uleran froze his movement halfway into his sitting position, and without lowering his body more, turned his head to frown at Thomas. The sheriff was a man nearly into his fourth decade of living. Solid and tough, his scarred and broken face was a testimony to much of his first three decades of the life of a fighting man. When he smiled, warmth spread from him as from a hearth. But when he set his face in anger—as it was now—ladies would gasp and children quiver.

Despite his worries, Thomas suddenly laughed.

"Relax, Robert. You'd think I had just pulled a dagger!"

"You may as well have, m'lord," Robert of Uleran grumbled. "To even suggest my men might shirk their duty."

Thomas continued to laugh. "My humblest apologies. How could I not think they had been searched?"

Satisfied, the big man finally eased himself onto the bench. "We searched them thrice. There is something about their procession which disturbs me. Even if they claim to be men of God."

Thomas raised an eyebrow. "Claim?"

Robert of Uleran nodded once. "They carry nothing except the usual travel bags. And a sealed vial. And a message for the Lord of Magnus."

"Vial," Thomas repeated thoughtfully.

"I like it not," Robert of Uleran scowled. "A vial which they claim holds the blood of a martyr."

Thomas snorted. "Simply another religious miracle designed to draw yet more money from even the most poverty-stricken.

To which martyr does this supposed relic belong?"

The sheriff stood and paced briefly before spinning on his heels. He looked directly into the eyes of Thomas, Lord of Magnus.

"Which martyr?" Robert of Uleran repeated softly. "The man who listened to the cock crow on the dawn of the crucifixion of Christ, the man Christ called the rock of the church more than 1,200 years ago. St. Peter himself."

3

Thomas called for the doors to the royal chamber to be opened. Normal chaos reigned in the large hall on the other side. The huge fire at the side of the hall crackled and hissed as the fat dripped down from the pig roasting on a spit above, and servants and maids scurried in all directions to prepare for the upcoming daily meal. Already, the high table—set across the far end of the hall on a raised platform—was ready with pewter plates in place. The rough wooden tables down the entire length of the hall—still empty of any food—were crowded with people, some resting as they waited to see Thomas, some merely there because of the liveliness of the hall. There were men armed with swords, bows, and large wolfhounds; there were women in fine dress and in rags.

Standing to the side of all this activity, aloof to the world, were fifteen men garbed in simple gowns of brown. They did not bother to look up—as did the rest in the hall—when the doors opened. When summoned by Robert of Uleran, two of the men broke away from the group, but walked as if agreeing to the summons was bestowing a favor.

Thomas, near the entrance of the chamber, noticed the posturing immediately, and gritted his teeth. Too often, holy men were this blatantly arrogant. Thomas wrapped his purple cloak around him, and crossed his arms and waited for their approach.

He said nothing as the doors swung shut again, leaving the two of them alone in the chamber with him and Robert of Uleran.

The silence hung heavy. Thomas made it no secret that he was inspecting them, although their loose clothing hid much. Thomas could not tell if they were soft and fat, or hardened athletes. He could only be certain that they were large men, both of them.

The first, who stared back at Thomas with black eyes of flint, had a broad, unlined forehead and a blond beard cropped short. His nostrils flared slightly with each breath, giving away his anger at the clear lack of trust shown by the Lord of Magnus.

The second appeared slightly older, perhaps because the skin of his face above a scraggly beard was etched with pockmarks. His eyes were flat and unreadable.

Each had shaved the top of his skull. Because the tight skin gleamed, Thomas guessed it was a very recent shave, or that they spent time each day to reshave.

Thomas fought a shiver. Something about their unblinking acceptance of his inspection suggested the idle laziness and superior vantage point of a cat unconcerned by the mouse trapped and looking upward from within its paws.

Thomas forced calmness upon his own features, and hoped his eyes in return seemed as cold and as gray as the North Sea only thirty miles to the east.

Unlike many of the men in Magnus, Thomas kept his hair

long. Tied back, it added strength to the impression immediately given through square shoulders, a high, intelligent forehead, and a straight noble nose.

Thomas had spent the entire winter learning and practicing sword play. The hall outside had rung again and again each day with the clang of steel against steel, and no man could handle a broadsword for hour after hour without developing considerable bulk.

Thus, at 15 years of age, Thomas had the size of mature men four or five years older. That—and the well fitted expensive clothing— added to the poise earned from the responsibilities which he carried as Lord of Magnus, and made him an imposing figure when he decided to withhold even the slightest of smiles.

He did not smile now.

Finally, the younger of the two men in front of him coughed.

It was enough of a sign of weakness for Thomas to speak at last. "You wished an audience."

"We come from afar, from—" the younger man began.

Thomas held up his hand and slowly and coldly stressed each word. "You wished an audience."

The older man coughed this time. "M'lord, we beg that you might grant us a brief moment to hear our request."

"Granted." Thomas smiled briefly and without warmth. "Make introduction."

"I am Hugh de Gainfort," the dark-haired man said. "My fellow clergyman is Edmund of Byrne."

Thomas stepped backward slowly until reaching his throne. He then sat upon it, leaned forward, and steepled his fingers in thought below his chin.

"Clergymen?" he said. "You appear to be neither Franciscan nor Cistercian monks. And representatives of Rome already serve Magnus."

Hugh shook his head. "We are from the true church. We are the Priests of the Holy Grail."

"Priests, I presume, in search of the Holy Grail." But even as he asked, Thomas felt a sudden chill to see their smug certainty.

Hugh's next words confirmed that chill, and came on the edge of his disdainful smile. "No. We guard the Holy Grail."

"Impossible!" blurted Robert of Uleran. "One might as well believe in King Arthur's sword in the stone."

For a moment, Hugh's eyes widened.

In shock? Yet, the moment passed so quickly that Thomas immediately doubted he had seen any reaction.

"The Grail and King Arthur's sword have much in common," Hugh replied with scorn. "And only fools believe that the passing of centuries can wash away the truth."

Robert of Uleran opened his mouth and drew a breath. Thomas held up his hand again to silence any argument.

"I am told that your procession brings a saint's relic," Thomas said. "Are you here among the people of Magnus—" Thomas raised his top lip in distaste "—to squeeze from them money and profit from the blood of St. Peter? Or have you requested audience merely to siphon directly from the treasury of Magnus?"

Edmund clucked as if Thomas were a naughty child. "We are not false priests. They shall be punished soon enough for their methods of leeching blood from the poor. No, we are here to preach the truth."

"Yes," Hugh added as humorlessly and dryly as if they were discussing a transaction of business accounts. "Our only duty is to deliver our message to whomever has the hunger for it. We have coin for our lodging in Magnus, so we beg no charity. Instead, we simply request that you allow us to speak freely among your people during our stay."

"If permission is refused?" Thomas asked.

Hugh bowed in a mocking gesture.

"Enough of your villagers have already heard rumors of the martyr's blood. You dare not refuse now." The priest's voice became silky with deadliness. "And if you do, our miracles will become your curses."

4

The Priests of the Holy Grail waited until the middle of the afternoon on their second day to demonstrate their first miracle.

The low gray clouds of the previous week had been broken by a sun so strong it almost felt like summer. To the villagers of Magnus, it was a good omen. These priests, it seemed, had banished the dismal spring chill

Now the streets were hectic with activity of men and women and children anxious to be out-of-doors and in the bright sunshine Shopkeepers shouted good-natured abuse at each other across the rapidly drying mud of the streets. Housewives forgot to barter down to the last farthing, often accepting the stated price with absent smiles as they enjoyed the heat of the sun on their shoulders. Servants shook bedding free of the winter's accumulation of fleas and dirt. Dogs lay sprawled at the sides of buildings, too lazy in the promise of summer to nose among the scrap heaps

The Priests of the Holy Grail were quick to take advantage of the general good spirits

There were only five now, speaking at the corner of the church building which dominated the center of Magnus. The others rested quietly within nearby shadows. They took turns in shifts, constantly calling out and delivering selected sermons, answering questions, and warding off insults from the less believing.

Hugh de Gainfort was leading this group of five into the hours of the early afternoon. His brown robe made him swelter in the heat; that much was obvious by the balls of oily sweat which poured down the slopes of his shaven skull.

Still he spoke with power. It was not unusual for twenty or thirty of the village people to be gathered in front at any given moment.

He looked beyond the crowd, into the shadows of the church, then nodded, so briefly that any observer would have doubted the action had been made.

"Miracles shall prove we are the bearers of God's truth." Hugh raised his voice without interrupting his sentence as he completed that slight nod, "AND AS PROMISED FOR TWO DAYS NOW, ONE SHALL NOW APPEAR"

His raised voice—and his promise—drew murmurs from the crowd in front, and attention from passersby

"Yes!" Hugh continued in the near shout. "Draw forward, believers and unbelievers of Magnus! Within the quarter hour, you shall witness the signs of a new age of truth!"

Hugh swept his arms in a circle. "Go," he urged the crowd. "Go now and return with friends and family! Go forth and bring back with you all those to be saved! For what you see will be a sure sign of blessing!"

The other four priests—all garbed in brown, and all with skulls shaven—began chanting, "The promised miracle shall deliver blessings to all who witness The promised miracle shall deliver blessings to all who witness."

For several seconds, none in the crowd reacted.

Hugh roared, "Go forth into Magnus! Return immediately but do not return alone! Go!"

An old man hobbled away. Then a housewife. Finally, the rest of the crowd turned, almost in unison, and spread in all directions. Some ran. Some walked and stumbled as they looked back at Hugh, as if afraid he might perform the miracle in their absence.

Almost immediately, Edmund of Byrne left the shadows. He carried a statue nearly half his height, and set it down carefully in front of Hugh.

"Well spoken, my good man." He patted the top of the statue. "Remember, Hugh, not until they are nearly in a frenzy, should you deliver. Thomas of Magnus must suffer the same fate as the Earl of York."

Edmund smiled with a savage gleam as he finished speaking. "After all, there is a certain sweetness in casting a man into his own dungeon."

5

Within half an hour a great, noisy crowd had filled the small square in front of the stone church. It was not often that such unexpected entertainment might break life's monotony and struggle.

Hugh de Gainfort raised his arms to request silence. Beneath bright sun, his pockmarks formed pebbled shadows across the skin of his face.

"People of Magnus," he called. "Many of you doubt the Priests of the Holy Grail. Some of you have ridiculed us yesterday and today—but we, the speakers of truth, forgive. After you witness the miracle of the Madonna, such insults will not be forgiven as ones delivered from ignorance. After today, none of you will be excused for not following our truth!"

Excited and disdainful murmurings arose from the crowd.

Hugh lifted the statue, and with seemingly little effort, held it high above him.

"Behold, the Madonna, the statue of the sainted Mother Mary."

The murmurings stopped instantly. All in the crowd strained for a better view.

The sun-whitened statue was of a woman with her head bowed behind a veil. A long flowing cape covered most of her body. Only her feet, clad in sandals, and her hands, folded in prayer, appeared from beneath the cape.

Few, though, ever remembered the details of folded hands or sandaled feet. The Madonna's face captivated, such were the carved details of exquisite agony. The Madonna's eyes were even more haunting than the pain etched so clearly in the plaster face. Those eyes were deep crystal, a luminous blue which seemed to search the heart of every person in the crowd.

"The Mother Mary herself knew well of the Holy Grail," Hugh said in deep, slow words as he set the statue down again. "She blessed this statue for our own priests those thirteen centuries ago, our own priests who already held the sacred Holy Grail. Thus, we were established first as the one true church!"

A voice, from the entrance to the church, interrupted Hugh. "This is not a story to be believed! Only the Holy Pope and the church of Rome may make such claim!"

Hugh turned slowly to face his challenger.

The thin man at the church entrance wore a loose black robe. His face was white with anger, his fists clenched at his sides.

"Ah!" Hugh proclaimed loudly for his large audience. "A representative of the oppressors of the people!"

This shift startled the priest. "Oppressors?"

"Oppressors!" Hugh's voice gained in resonance, as if here were a trained actor. "You have set the rules according to a religion of convenience! A religion designed to give priests and kings control over the people!"

The priest stood on his toes in rage. "This . . . is . . . vile!" he said with a strained scream. "Someone call the Lord of Magnus!"

No one in the crowd moved.

Hugh smiled, a wolf moving in on the helpless fawn.

"The truth shall speak for itself," Hugh said. He turned back to the people. "Shall we put truth to the test?"

"Yes!" came the shout. "Truth to the test!"

The priest felt the trap shut. He knew he could not defy such a large crowd, and he felt a fear at Hugh's confidence.

Hugh held up his arms again. Immediate silence followed.

"What say you?" Hugh queried the priest without deigning to glance back. "Or have you fear of the results?"

More long silence. Finally the priest croaked, "I have no fear."

Hugh smiled at the crowd in front of him. He noted their flushed faces, their concentration on his words.

Yes, he mentally licked his lips, *they are ready*.

"This Madonna," he said with a theatrical flourish, "blessed by the Mother Mary herself, shall tell us the truth. Let us take her inside the church. If the priest speaks truth, the Madonna will remain as she is. However, if in this church resides falseness against God, the Madonna will weep in sadness!"

Even as Hugh finished speaking, those at the back of the crowd began to push forward. Excited babble washed over all of them. None wanted to miss the test.

Once again, Hugh was forced to request silence.

"And," he continued in those confident, deep tones, "when the truth is revealed, the new and faithful followers of the Priests of the Holy Grail will soon be led to the Grail itself!"

At this, not even Hugh's upraised arms could stop the avalanche of shouting. The legendary Grail promised blessings to all who touched it!

Knowing nothing more could be said above the tumult, Hugh took the statue into his arms, and spun around to face the church. He marched forward.

Without pausing to acknowledge the priest, he walked through the deep shadows of the church's entrance, and into the quiet coolness beyond.

Hugh kept walking until he reached the altar at the front. He cleared the lit candles, and set the statue down, making sure it faced the wooden pews.

Soon the church was full. Every eye strained to see the Madonna's face. Every throat was dry with expectation.

"Dear Mother Mary," Hugh cried to the curved ceiling above, "is this a house worthy of your presence?"

The statue, of course, remained mute. So skillful, however, was Hugh's performance, that some in the audience expected a reply.

Hugh fell to his knees and clasped his hands and begged at the statue's feet.

"Dear Mother Mary," Hugh cried again, "is this a house worthy of your presence?"

For a dozen heartbeats, he stayed on his knees, silent, head bowed, hands clasped high above him. Then he looked upward at the statue and moaned.

He stood in triumph and pointed.

"Behold," he shouted, "the Madonna weeps."

Three elderly women in the front rows fainted. Grown men crossed themselves. Mothers wept in terror. And all stared in horror and fascination at the statue.

Even in the dimly filtered light at the front of the church, water visibly glistened from the Madonna's eyes. As each second passed, another large drop broke from each eye and slowly rolled downward.

6

Thomas made it his custom to greet each dawn from the eastern ramparts of the castle walls.

At that hour, the wind had yet to rise on the moors. Often, mist would rise from the lake that surrounded Magnus, and behind Thomas, the town would lay silent as he lost himself in thoughts and absorbed the beauty of the sun's rays breaking over the tops of the faraway hills to cut sharp shadows into the dips and swells of the land.

There, on the ramparts in the quiet of a new day, Thomas found great solace in prayer—not the rituals intoned by priests who insisted only they could mediate between man and God— but the opening of his heart to the God Thomas knew listened directly to each man and woman who called upon His name.

Yes, Thomas now took comfort in his faith, something he would not have believed possible a year earlier; but he still could not overcome his suspicion of the priests and monks who carried and used religion as a battering ram for their own selfish purposes.

For many, the church was more of a career than a way to serve God. Thomas well knew his society was classified in three orders: those who work, the peasants; those who fight, the nobility; and those who pray, the clergy.

Since praying was easier than work, and safer than fighting, it was an attractive career. Because of this—as Thomas remembered too well from his days as an orphan in the supposed care of monks—many abused their positions of power. The leaders in the church were as prone as the nobles to entertain in halls off plates of gold and silver. The clergy—using the hard-earned money of their peasant charges—often wore jewels and rings and kept fine horses and expensive hounds and hawks.

It was not difficult to claim shelter in the wings of the Roman church. A test for clerical status was simple—because literacy and education were so rare, any man who could read a Latin text from the Bible could claim "benefit of clergy." This was especially valuable, for those in the church who had committed a crime—from simple theft to blatant murder—were given complete exemption from the courts of the land. In this manner, clergymen escaped the king's judges. And, since the laws within the church forbade the use of mutilation and the death sentence and, since it was too expensive for the church to maintain its own prisons, it relied on spiritual penalties for punishment. At the very worst, a cleric might face a fine, or a light whipping for even the most terrible of crimes.

Thus, Thomas lived in uneasy alliance with the priests of Magnus. Because no matter how powerful any ruler, the power of the church was equal. More dreaded to an earl or king than a sieging army was the threat of excommunication. After all, if the mass of people believed that a ruler's power was given directly by God, how could that ruler maintain power if the church made him an outcast?

So, each Sabbath, Thomas entered the church to worship as

expected by tradition. Too often, however, his mind wandered. Unlike most of the people of Magnus, Thomas could read and write. He understood Latin in its written form, and winced at the biblical inaccuracies spouted by priests too willing to deliver whatever message it took to ensure the ignorant peasants remained cowed by the threat of God's punishment.

It was with relief, then, that Thomas pursued the knowledge of God through his own reading and his own prayers each dawn.

And without fail, each morning following his prayers—as he did each night before falling to sleep—Thomas would silently ask himself the questions which haunted him, in empty hopes that so asking might one day deliver an answer.

An old man once cast the sun into darkness and directed me here from the gallows where a knight was about to die, falsely accused. The old man—even back then—knew my dream of conquering Magnus. Who was that old man? How did he know?

A valiant and scarred knight befriended me and helped me win the castle that once belonged to his own lord. Then departed. Why?

A crooked candlemaker and Isabelle, the daughter of the lord we vanquished, were captured and imprisoned in the dungeons of Magnus, yet escaped in a manner still unknown. How?

The midnight messenger, Katherine? She spent all those years in Magnus disguised beneath bandages as a scarred freak. Was she one of the false sorcerers who nearly won from me Magnus? Or was she truly a friend, now banished unfairly by my command from this kingdom?

And what is the secret of Magnus?

The early rays of sun which warmed Thomas on the eastern ramparts had never replied to these silent questions.

On this day, less than a week after the arrival of the Priests of the Holy Grail, Thomas now had other urgent questions and problems to occupy him as he walked the ramparts.

Not even the enthusiastically squirming burden left in his

throne room yesterday—Thomas smiled as he recalled how Tiny John had deposited a clumsy puppy on his lap—was enough of a distraction during these terrible days.

His only comfort was in knowing that there was one man, of low position, in all of Magnus who had a calming and gentle wisdom. It took little for Thomas to decide that this day required another visit and discussion.

"Five days of nonsense about the Holy Grail!" exploded Thomas. "Blood of a martyr which clots and unclots as directed by prayer! I am at my wit's end, Gervase. It is almost enough for me to sympathize with the priests of Rome."

"Then the matter must be grave," the elderly man, on his knees in the rich dirt of the garden, chuckled without looking up from his task. "Brave would be the man to gamble that you ever side with Rome."

Thomas paced two steps past Gervase on the stone path which meandered through the garden, then whirled and paced back. "Jest if you will, but do not be surprised if you find yourself without gainful work when the priests you serve are cast from this very church."

Gervase merely hummed in the sunshine which covered his stooped shoulders in pleasant warmth. His gray hair was combed straight back. His voice was deep and rich in tone, and matched in strength the lines of humor and character etched in his face. He had thick, gnarled fingers, as capable of threading the most delicate needles as of clawing among the roots of the roughest bush, which he did now with great patience.

Carefully pruned bushes stood tall among wide low shrubs, and lined in front of these were rows of flowers almost ready to bloom. The greatest treasure for Gervase among these were his roses. He would coax forth each summer the petals of white, or of pink, or of yellow, all considered prizes of delight by the noble women of Magnus.

Gervase gently snapped another weed free from the roots of a rosebush. He placed the weed on a rapidly drying pile an arm's length away. "The sun proves itself to be quite hot these days," he said in a leisurely tone. "It does wonders for these precious plants. Unfortunately, it also encourages the weeds."

Thomas sighed. "Gervase, do you not understand what happens within Magnus? With these signs of miracles, the Priests of the Holy Grail have almost the entire population of Magnus in their grip."

Gervase straightened with effort, then finally turned to regard the young master of Magnus.

"I understand it is much too late to prevent what surely must happen next. The horse has escaped the barn, Thomas. Therefore, I will not worry about closing the gate." Gervase swept his arms in a broad motion to indicate the garden. "So I shall direct my efforts where they will have affect."

Thomas stopped halfway through another stride. "So you agree with me," he accused "And what do you believe will happen next?"

"The Priests of the Holy Grail will replace those within the church now," Gervase said mildly. "Then, I suspect, from the pulpit they will preach sedition."

"Sedition? Rebellion against the established order?" Thomas exploded again. "Impossible. To set their hand against the church is one thing, but against the royal order is yet another!"

Gervase shook the dirt from his knees and walked to a bench half hidden by overhanging branches.

Thomas followed

"Impossible?" Gervase echoed softly as he sat. "Last summer you conquered Magnus, and delivered all of us from the oppression of our former master. Yet how have you spent your winter? Relaxed and unafraid?"

Thomas sat alongside the old man. He did not answer immediately. Around them echoed the joyful caroling of the birds of spring, oblivious to the matters of state now in discussion between an old caretaker and a young lord.

"You know the opposite," Thomas said slowly, knowing where his answer would lead. "Day after day, each meal, each glass of wine is tasted first for poison by the official tester. Each visitor is searched thoroughly for daggers or other hidden weapons before an audience with me. Double guards are posted at the door to my bedchamber each night. Guards man the entrance to this garden, ready to protect me at the slightest alarm. I am a prisoner within my own castle."

"Why?" Gervase asked.

"You know full well," Thomas replied. "After I reconquered this castle, the real enemies appeared—Druids, those secret and false sorcerers. Despite another victory over their next attempt, I believe the Druids still threaten at each turn—invisible and deadly."

"Thus," Gervase said with no trace of triumph, "you are no stranger to rebellion. Why, then, do you persist in thinking it may not come from another source?"

"Perhaps," Thomas countered. "Yet these are priests against priests, Holy Grail against those from Rome, each seeking authority in religious matters, not matters of state."

Thomas let his voice trail away as Gervase shook his head and pursed his lips in a frown. "Thomas, these new priests carry powerful weapons! The Weeping Madonna. The blood of St Peter. And the promise of the Holy Grail."

Gervase paused, then said, "Thomas, tell me, should the Priests of the Holy Grail become your enemy, how would you fight them?"

Thomas opened his mouth to retort, then slowly shut it as he realized the implications.

"Yes," Gervase said, "pray these men do not seek your power. For they cannot be fought by sword. Every man, woman, and child within Magnus would turn against you."

7

Thomas leaned on the ledge near the window, and waited until Robert of Uleran had entered and closed the door to the bedchamber.

"Attack, beast!" Thomas called out. "Attack!"

With a high-pitched yipping, the puppy bolted from beneath a bench and flung itself with enthusiasm at Robert's ankle.

"Spare me, m'lord!" cried Robert of Uleran in fake terror. "Spare me from this savage monster!"

The puppy had a firm grip on the leather upper of Robert's boot, and no shaking could free him.

Thomas laughed so hard that he could barely speak. "Tickle him behind the ears, good Robert. He's an easy one to fool."

Robert of Uleran reached down, then stopped and glared at Thomas with suspicion. "He'll not piddle on my boot instead?"

"You guessed my secret weapon," Thomas hooted. Tiny John's gift had already proven itself as dangerous.

"Bah." Robert of Uleran reached down, soothed the puppy with soft words and a gentle touch, then scooped him up and quickly dropped him in Thomas' arms.

"Go on," Robert of Uleran said to the puppy. "Now discharge your royal duties. Then we'll see who has the last laugh."

"Rich jest," Thomas said, and cradled the dog in the crook of his right arm. He rubbed the top of the puppy's head thoughtfully. "Would that all of Magnus could be tamed this easily."

Robert of Uleran nodded, then spoke above the panting of the puppy. "You seem far from ill, m'lord. The reports had led me to believe I would find you half dead beneath the covers of your bed."

Thomas smiled. "I was that convincing, was I? Of course, to lie fully dressed beneath those covers is enough to put the sweat of fever on any person's brow."

Thomas became serious very quickly. "Do not let the rumor rest. It serves our purpose for all to believe the fever grips me so badly that I cannot leave this room."

"M'lord?"

"Robert, three days ago—with the miracle of the weeping statue—the priests of the Holy Grail won the mantle of authority in the church of Magnus. They preach now openly from the pulpit itself and the former priests have been banished from the church. It is not a good sign."

"It cannot be bad," Robert protested. "Let the religious orders fight among themselves."

"I wish I could agree," Thomas said. The puppy chewed on the end of his sleeve and sighed with satisfaction. "But I must be sure that there is no threat to the rest of Magnus."

Robert of Uleran raised his eyebrows in a silent question.

"All winter," Thomas continued, "we have been hidden in these towers, away from the people. Aside from the servants in this keep, and those who request audience, I have almost been a prisoner."

"The Druids, m'lord," Robert of Uleran said in a whisper.

"You cannot be blamed for precautions."

"Perhaps not. But now I have little idea what concerns these people in everyday life. For certes, I hear their legal problems in the throne room, but little else."

"But—"

"But how do they feel about these new priests?" Thomas interrupted. "Someone must go among them and discover this."

Robert of Uleran straightened. "I will send someone immediately."

"A guard?" Thomas asked. "A knight? Do you believe such a man will receive the confidence of housewives and beggars?"

Robert of Uleran slowly shook his head.

Thomas grinned. "I thought you might agree. Therefore, someone must spend a day on the streets in disguise, perhaps as a beggar himself."

"But who, m'lord? It must be someone we trust. And I am too large and well known for such a task."

"Who do I trust better than myself?" Thomas countered. His grin widened. "And it has been a long and terrible winter cooped inside these walls."

8

Thomas rejoiced to be a beggar.

Gone, indeed, was the long, flowing purple cape he wore publicly as Lord of Magnus. Gone were the soft linen underclothing, the rings, the sword and scabbard that went with his position.

In their stead were coarse dirty rags for clothing, no jewelry, and—as Thomas had copied from a long departed knight friend—a short sword ingeniously hidden in a sheath strapped behind him, between his shoulder blades. To pull the sword free, Thomas would only have to reach over his shoulders as if scratching his back.

With Robert of Uleran's help, Thomas had dyed his skin several shades darker with the juice of boiled bark. This, he hoped, would give him the rough texture and appearance of a person who spent too much time outside in the bitter cold wind or the baking sun.

Thomas had cut his hair short in ragged patches, and also carefully scraped dark grease repeatedly with his hands to

impact the filth beneath his fingernails. It was his plan to spend
at least two days among the peasants of Magnus, and only the
blindest of fools would fail to notice the improbability of clean
hands on a street beggar.

But how would Thomas disguise his features?

Robert of Uleran had suggested an eyepatch. Many in the
land were disfigured or crippled, and many of those by necessi-
ty were forced to beg or die. True, it was not common, yet it was
not unusual for another strange beggar with only one eye to
appear among the poor.

Thus disguised, Thomas let his shoulders sag and added a
limp as he slipped unnoticed through the great banquet hall
among the crowds of morning visitors.

He stepped into the spring air outside, and rejoiced at his
freedom as a beggar. For with his purple cloak and scepter of
authority, he had also left behind responsibilities and the con-
stant vigil against Druid assassination.

It took less than a minute for some of that joy to be tarnished.

"Step aside, scum!" bellowed a large man guiding a mule
loaded with leather. When Thomas did not react instantly —
indeed, he was wondering with amusement which poor scum
the man meant — the large man shoved him rudely back into a
crowd of people on the side of the street.

"Watch yourself!" another shouted at Thomas. Hands grasped
and pulled at him, while other hands pushed him away in disgust. One well-placed kick inside the back of his knee almost
pitched Thomas forward, and when he stood upright again, he
knew it would not be difficult to fake his limp for the rest of the
day.

Thomas moved ahead, handicapped by the lack of depth of
vision forced upon him by the use of only one eye.

Still, he refused to be downcast. He was, after all, temporarily
free. In two days, he would resume his position of authority

again—without regrets, of course—but for now, he could wander much as he did the first time he had set foot in Magnus as a powerless orphan.

He smiled to himself to remember that day. The streets, of course, looked identical. Shops crowded the streets so badly that the more crooked buildings actually touched roofs where they leaned into each other. Space among the people who bustled in front of him was equally difficult to find.

Since so few could read, colorfully painted symbols on signs identified the trades of each shop. The apothecary sign—which carried potions and herbs and medicines—displayed three gilded pills. A bush sketched in dark shades marked the vintner, or wine shop. A horse's head—the harness maker. A unicorn—the goldsmith. A white arm with stripes—the surgeon barber. The potter, the skinner, the shoemaker, the beer seller, baker, and butcher all carried distinct signs.

Thomas did not let his renewed sightseeing stop him from carefully placing each new—and limped—footstep. The streets were filled with the stench and mess of emptied chamberpots and the waste of sheep or calf or pig innards thrown there by the butchers.

Pigs squealed, donkeys brayed in protest against heavy carts, and dogs barked, all a backdrop of noise against the hum of people busy in the sunshine.

Thomas sighed and turned backward to squint against that sunshine as he gazed at the large keep of Magnus that dominated the center of the village. It was easy to rejoice in his new role as beggar, knowing he would be back in its quiet and safety by the next evening, and knowing he would not need to beg to feed himself.

To confirm that, Thomas reached for his hidden pouch which contained two silver coins. Beggar or not, he did not relish going hungry in the eve or the morrow's—

Thomas groaned.

Those grasping hands in the crowd! Only five minutes away from the castle and he had been picked as clean as a country fool.

Thomas then sighed and resigned himself to a long two days among his people.

" 'Tis our good fortune the weather holds so well," the old lady cackled to Thomas. "Or the night would promise us much worse than empty bellies. The roof above us leaks horribly in any rain at all."

Thomas grunted.

The old lady chose to accept his grunt as one of agreement. She moved herself closer to Thomas and snuggled against his side in the straw.

Thomas grunted again, then fought the urge to laugh aloud.

Which was worse? The cloying barnyard smell of the dirty stable straw, or the stale, unwashed odor of the old woman who sought him for warmth. His skin prickled; already he could feel, or imagine he felt, the fleas transferring from the old woman to him.

Besides, Thomas did not know if he agreed with her or not. It had been so long since he had felt this hunger, he almost would have preferred a rainy cold night for the sake of being fed.

He stared into the darkness around him. Vague shapes moved; those horses, at least, were content.

The old woman burped, releasing a sour gas which did little to help Thomas sleep.

"I wonder," he asked, "why there are not more of us seeking shelter here in the stables. Do they fear the soldiers of Magnus?"

Thomas, however, knew well the answer to that. As lord, he had commanded his men not to harry the poor who commonly used the stables as a last resort.

The old woman snorted. "The others choose the church as sanctuary."

"Ah," Thomas said. He maintained his role as a wandering beggar, new to Magnus. "I had heard the priests of Magnus would give food and a roof to any who pledged work the following day."

Thomas smiled quickly to himself as he finished his words. After all, he and Gervase had set that policy themselves, to allow the penniless their pride, and to stop the abuse of charity by the lazy.

Much to his surprise, the old woman laughed a cruel laugh. "No longer! Have you not heard? Those priests have been replaced by the men of the Holy Grail."

"Indeed," Thomas replied.

"Indeed." The old woman explained the miracle of the weeping statue and its affect on the people of Magnus, and how the Priests of the Holy Grail had ruthlessly used that newfound power to banish the former priests from their very own church building.

"I understand little, then," Thomas admitted. "You say the priests of old are not in the church. Where, then, do the less fortunate stay each night, if not here in the stables or at the church?"

The old woman shifted, heedless of the elbow which forced a gasp from Thomas.

"I did not say the church was empty," she told him. "Only that the poor need not pledge a day's services in exchange for food and lodging. Instead, the Priests of the Holy Grail demand an oath of loyalty"

"What!" Thomas sat bolt upright and bumped the woman solidly. He almost forgot himself in his outrage. He forced himself to relax again

"Lad," the old woman admonished. "I prithee might give warning the next time. My old bones cannot take such movement."

"I beg pardon," Thomas said, much more quietly. "It seems such a strange requirement, this pledging an oath." He must keep his voice wondering instead of angry. "I had thought, however, an oath of loyalty could only be pledged to those who rule."

The old woman cackled again. "Are you so fresh from the countryside that your eyes and ears have been plugged with manure? These priests have promised the Holy Grail to their followers. With such power, how could they not rule soon?"

9

Once again, Thomas fought frustration at the invincibility of his unreachable opponents. When he felt he could speak calmly again, he pretended little interest.

"What do you know of this Grail?" he asked casually. "And its power therein?"

The old woman clutched Thomas tighter as the evening chill settled upon them.

"Had you no parents, lad? Anyone to instruct you in common legends?"

She reacted instantly to his sudden stillness.

"It is my turn to beg pardon," she said softly "There are too many orphans in the land."

" 'Tis nothing." Thomas waved a hand in the darkness, as if brushing away memories. "You spoke of the Holy Grail."

"The Holy Grail," she repeated. "A story to pass the time of any night."

Her voice became singsong, oddly beautiful as it dropped into a storytelling chant. As Thomas listened, the stable around him seemed faraway. He no longer sucked the air carefully between his teeth to lessen the stench. The straw no longer stabbed him in tiny pinpricks. And the burden of the woman leaning against him lessened. Thomas let himself be carried away by her voice, back through lost centuries to the Round Table of King Arthur's court.

"Long ago," she said softly, "at Camelot, there was a fellow-ship of knights so noble . . . "

So the story began.

It was a quest for the eternal, she explained, this legendary search by King Arthur's knights for the Holy Grail. The tiny, wrinkled woman recounted the legend which so many in the land wanted to believe.

The Holy Grail, she told Thomas, was the cup which Christ had used at the Last Supper, the night before He was to be crucified. This cup was later obtained by a wealthy Jew, Joseph of Arimathaea, who undertook to care for Christ's body before burial. When Christ's body disappeared after the third day in the tomb, Joseph was accused of stealing it and was thrown into prison and deprived of food, but miraculously kept alive by a dove which entered his cell every day and deposited a wafer into the cup.

"Yes," the old woman breathed, "it was in that prison cell that Christ Himself appeared in a blaze of light and entrusted the cup to Joseph's care! It was then that Christ instructed Joseph in the mystery of the Lord's Supper and in certain other secrets! It is those secrets which make the Holy Grail so powerful!"

"These secrets?" Thomas interrupted.

"No one knows," she said. "But it matters little. How can these secrets not help but be marvelous!"

Yes, Thomas thought sourly, *despite the profound lack of biblical truth in this legend, it is something to which the people want to cling, and oddly, again I find myself sympathizing with the difficulties of the church as it struggles to counteract the ignorance around it in this age of darkness.*

Thomas did not betray that almost bitter reaction. He wanted the old woman to continue, wanted badly to know if the Priests of the Holy Grail had managed to poison the people of Magnus entirely.

She told him the rest of the legend in awed tones, as if whispered words in the black of the stable might reach those priests of power.

Joseph was released in A.D. 70, she informed Thomas, and was joined by his sister and her husband Bron and a small group of followers. They traveled overseas into exile—careful to guard the cup on their journey—and formed the First Table of the Holy Grail.

"This table was meant to represent the Table of the Last Supper," the old woman said with reverence. "One seat was always empty, the seat which represented Judas, the betrayer. A member of the company once tried sitting there and was swallowed up by the earth!"

Thomas marveled at the woman's superstitious belief. Yet, he told himself, if one cannot read, one cannot combat the evils of ignorance.

"Go on," he said gently. "This takes place long before King Arthur, does it not?"

"Oh yes," she said quickly. "Joseph of Arimathaea sailed here to our great island and set up the first Christian church at Glastonbury, and somewhere nearby the Grail Castle."

She sighed. "Alas, in time the Grail Keeper lost his faith, and the entire land around the castle became barren and known as the Waste Land, and strangely, could not be reached by travellers. The land—and the Grail—remained lost for many generations."

The woman settled farther. Her silence continued for so long that Thomas suspected she had fallen asleep.

"Until King Arthur?" he prompted.

"No need to hurry me," she said almost crossly. "I had closed my eyes to see in my mind those noble knights of yesteryear. Too few are pleasant thoughts for an old forgotten woman."

Then, remembering the impatience of youth, she patted Thomas' knee in forgiveness. "Yes, lad. Until King Arthur. At the Round Table, the Holy Grail appeared once, floating veiled in a beam of sunlight, and those great knights pledged themselves to go in search of it."

Thomas settled back for a long story. Many were the escapades of King Arthur and his men, many the adventures in search of the Holy Grail, and many were the hours passed by people in its telling and retelling.

Thomas heard again of the perilous tests faced by Sir Lancelot, and his son Sir Galahad, Sir Bors, Sir Perceval, and the others. Thomas heard again how Sir Perceval, after wandering for five years in the wilderness, found the Holy Grail and healed the Grail Keeper, making the Waste Lands once again flower. Thomas heard again how Perceval, Galahad, and Bors then continued their journey until reaching a Heavenly City in the East, where they learned the mysterious secrets of the Grail and saw it taken into heaven.

She told it well, this legend which captured all imaginations. But she did not finish where the legend usually ended.

"And now," she said, "these priests offer to us the blood of a martyr of ancient times, blood which clots, then unclots after their prayer. They offer us the weeping statue of the Mother Mary. And they speak intimately of the Holy Grail, returned rightfully to them, with its powers to be shared among their followers!"

Thomas felt his chest grow tight. Indeed, these were the rumors he had feared. "These followers," he said cautiously, "what must they do to receive the benefits of the Holy Grail?"

The old woman clucked. "The same as the poor must do to receive shelter. Pledge an oath of loyalty, one that surpasses loyalty to the Lord of Magnus or any other earthly lord."

Open sedition, open rebellion! These were the rumors which had not yet reached him, the rumors he had sought by leaving his castle keep. How much time on his return did he have left to combat these priests?

Another thought struck Thomas.

"Yet you are here," Thomas said into the darkness to the woman curled against his side. "Here in the stable and not at the church. Why have you not pledged loyalty to this great power for the benefits of food and lodging?"

The old woman sighed. "An oath of loyalty is not one to be pledged lightly. And many years ago—when I had beauty and dreams—I pledged mine to the former Lord of Magnus."

"Yet . . . yet . . . " Thomas stammered suddenly at her impossible words, "was that not the lord which oppressed Magnus so cruelly, the one which Thomas the Boy Warrior so recently overcame?"

"You know much for a wandering beggar," she said sharply. "Especially for one ignorant of the Holy Grail."

"I have heard much in my first day here," Thomas countered quickly.

"So be it," the old woman agreed, then continued. "I did not swear an oath to that tyrant. No, my pledge of loyalty was given to the lord who reigned twenty years earlier, a kinder lord who lost Magnus to the tyrant."

Thomas marveled. This woman showed great loyalty to the same lord Thomas had avenged by reconquering Magnus. Yes, Thomas thought, *he would reward the old woman later, when he left disguise and resumed his duties as Lord of Magnus.*

He was given no time to ponder further.

The nearby horses stamped nervously at a sudden rustling at the entrance to the stable.

"Hide beneath the straw!" the old woman hissed. "We'll not be found!"

She began to burrow.

While Thomas did not share her fear, he wanted to maintain his role as a half-blind beggar, and a half-blind beggar in a strange town would do as she instructed. So he burrowed with her until they were nearly covered.

Many moments passed. Strangely, a small whimpering reached them.

Straw poked in Thomas' ears and closed eyes. Despite his curiosity, he held himself perfectly still.

Somehow, a patter of light footsteps approached their hiding spot directly and with no hesitation. From nowhere, a cold wet object bumped against his nose, and Thomas nearly yelped with surprise. Then a warm tongue rasped against his face, and Thomas recognized the intruder was nothing more alarming than a friendly puppy.

Could it be—

"Thomas?" a voice called.

Tiny John! What meaning did this hold?

Thomas sat up, and shook the straw free from his clothes. Yes, it was his puppy, and it wriggled against him in joy.

"I am here," Thomas said from beneath the straw. He ignored the surprised flinch of the old woman. "What urgent business brings you in pursuit?"

"I followed the puppy to you," Tiny John explained. "Exactly as Robert of Uleran predicted in his last words to me."

Thomas stood, quickly and with a cold lump of fear in his stomach.

"His *last* words? What has occurred?"

Tiny John's voice trembled. "The castle has fallen without a fight, m'lord. Few were those who dared resist the Priests of the Holy Grail."

1 0

"That . . . cannot . . . be," Thomas uttered. He felt weak on his legs.

"I recognize you!" the old woman cried as she stood beside Thomas.

"The deception could not be helped," Thomas muttered as his mind tried to grasp the impossible.

The old woman clouted Thomas. "Not you, ragamuffin! The boy. Dark as it is, I know his voice. Tiny John. He is a friend of the Lord of Magnus! And a friend to the poor. Why, more than once he has raided the banquet hall and brought us sweetmeats and flagons of wine. The boy could pick a bird clean of its feathers and not wake it from its perch. Why, he—"

The old woman's voice quavered, then faded. "What deception? You spoke of deception?" Then a quiet gasp of comprehension. "The boy called you Thomas! Not our Thomas? The Lord of Magnus?"

"Aye, indeed. I am Thomas. And by Tiny John's account, now the *former* Lord of Magnus."

The old woman groaned and sat heavily.

"M'lord," Tiny John blurted. "The priests appeared within the castle as if from the very walls! Like hordes of rats. They—"

"Robert of Uleran," Thomas interrupted with a leaden voice. He wanted to sit beside the old woman and, along with her, moan in low tones. "How did he die?"

"Die?"

"You informed me that he spoke his last words."

"Last words to *me*, m'lord. Guards were falling in all directions, slapping themselves as they fell! The priests claimed it was the hand of God, and for all to lay down their arms. It was then that Robert of Uleran pushed this puppy into my arms and told me to flee, told me to give you warning so that you would not return to the castle."

Thomas shifted the puppy into the crook of his left arm, and gripped Tiny John's shoulder fiercely with his right hand. "You know not the fate of Robert of Uleran?"

"No, m'lord. There was great confusion."

Thomas then covered his face with his free hand, and bowed his head in thought.

1 1

The shadows of the castle spires had hardly darkened with the rising sun, yet already the news was old.

Magnus has fallen to the Priests of the Holy Grail!

Some rejoiced, almost in religious ecstasy. After all, there had been the miracles of the weeping statue! The blood of the martyr! And now, stories of how the guards had fallen without a fight! Surely, the Grail must appear next!

Others were saddened. Wisely, they did not show this sadness, for who could guess the intentions of Magnus' new masters? Yet they grieved for the loss of Thomas, whom—they were told—had mysteriously vanished as the castle fell to the priests. These mourners were those who understood how Thomas had ruled with compassion and intelligence. These mourners were those who still had gratitude for the manner in which Thomas had released them from the bondage of a cruel lord less than a year before.

And few, although too many, were those whose eyes glinted with greed to hear that Thomas had been deposed. For the

Priests of the Holy Grail had offered a brick of the purest gold to the man who might capture Thomas.

Thomas limped along the edge of the streets. It took little effort to add that limp to his step; yesterday's brutal kick was this day's growing bruise, and a sleepless chilled night had stiffened his leg considerably.

Beneath his rags, he carried the puppy in the crook of his left arm. There was comfort in the warm softness of the animal against his skin. Occasionally, the puppy would lick Thomas' arm, something which each time brought a small smile, despite his troubles.

The smile did not reach anyone, however. Thomas kept his gaze lowered each halting step along the street. Whispers of the massive bounty placed upon his head had reached his ears too. *If the wrong sharp pair of eyes recognized him despite the rags and eyepatch, if the old woman did not keep her vow of secrecy, if Tiny John were to be captured by bounty hunters . .*

Yet Thomas could not remain hidden, cowed in a dark shadow somewhere within Magnus. If he were to survive, he must escape the castle island. To escape, he needed help from the one person he might trust

And to reach that person, he must enter directly the lion's den. So Thomas shuffled and limped to the edge of the church building, and prayed no Holy Grail priest would inquire too closely into the business of a starving beggar.

At the rear of the stone building, Thomas then followed the same garden path he had walked—was it only two days before?—so proudly in his purple cape as Lord of Magnus.

He rounded a bend of the path and saw the familiar figure of Gervase kneeling in the soil, pulling weeds with methodical delicacy. Thomas almost straightened and cried aloud in relief, but something stopped him.

What was this strangeness?

Not weeds, but piled in neat bundles beside Gervase were the rose bushes, roots already wilting in the sun. These were the most precious plants in the garden. *Why would Gervase weed them so diligently?*

Thomas sucked in his breath. Was this a message?

It disturbed Thomas enough, so that instead of a joyful call, Thomas continued to limp, and in that manner slowly reached the old man.

"Good sir," Thomas croaked. "Alms for the poor? I've not eaten in two days."

Gervase yanked another rosebush free from the soil and did not look up.

"Gervase," Thomas hissed. "It is I!"

The old man laid the bush on the nearest bundle and shuffled sideways on his knees to an unworked patch of soil.

"Of course it is you, Thomas. And not a moment too soon," Gervase grumbled without looking up. "Removing these roses has robbed me of five years of toil. This price counts little, however, for indeed you noticed and took it as warning."

Gervase paused, then said, "Ask your question again, as if I am deaf. And add insult to your words."

Thomas hesitated a moment, then raised his voice. "Are you deaf, you old cur? I've not eaten in two days."

"Do as the other beggars," Gervase instructed equally loudly with acted impatience. "Enter the church, and pledge allegiance to the Priests of the Holy Grail."

"Within the church?" Thomas said quickly. Shock raised his voice another level. "Why would—"

Thomas stopped abruptly as Gervase turned his head to look upward in response.

The mangled right side of the old man's face was swollen purple. Lines of dried blood showed the trails of cruel deep slashes. His right eye was swelled shut, and his nose was bent and pushed sideways at an angle which made Thomas gag.

"The Priests of the Grail know you and I are friends," Gervase said calmly without moving his head. "This was done to encourage me to deliver you into their hands. And as you may have guessed, they observe me now from the church windows and from the trees behind you."

Thomas blinked back tears.

"If you do not go into the church shortly," Gervase said in a continued low voice, "those watchers will suspect you and hunt you down. They may be within hearing distance. Ask me now which priest to see. Do not forget the insults."

Thomas hoped his voice would not choke as he forced the words into a scornful snarl. "Worthless donkey! Instruct me well the priest to seek, ere I add to the scars on your face!"

"Enter the church without hesitation," Gervase commanded quietly. "You *must* reach the altar. Then—" Gervase looked past Thomas, then back at Thomas. "Spit upon me. Curse me as if I have not replied!"

"I cannot."

"Thomas, anything to deceive our watchers. It will purchase a few precious moments."

The old man's eyes compelled Thomas.

"May the pox blind you and your children." Thomas finally blurted, then spat downward. "Feed my belly, not my ears, you miserable old man. May worms rot your flesh as you sleep if you do not help me."

Gervase recoiled and bowed his head as if afraid.

But his voice continued strong. "Thomas, the panel beneath the side of the altar which holds the candles, kick it sharply near the bottom. Twice. It will open. Use the passage for escape."

"But—"

Gervase then looked Thomas squarely in the eyes. Exhaustion and strain marked the other side of the old man's face. "After sixty steps, you must make the leap of faith. Understand? Make the leap of faith. You will find the knowledge you need near the burning water."

Thomas began to shake his head. "Burning water? What kind of madness do you—"

"Strike me across the face," Gervase urged Thomas. "You must reach the altar. If they suspect who you are, Magnus and all its history is lost."

"Gervase," Thomas pleaded.

Gervase sighed, "Show courage, my young friend. Strike me."

Thomas raised his right hand.

Gervase nodded slightly without turning away. "God be with you, Thomas," he whispered.

Thomas swung down. The impact of hand against swollen face sickened him. And the grunt of pain from the old man brought a whine from the covered puppy in Thomas' other arm.

Gervase crumpled beneath the blow.

Would that convince the unseen watchers?

Thomas stepped over Gervase, then limped onward, toward the entrance of the church.

He kept his head low and wept.

12

At the wide doors to the church, Thomas discovered some of his fears had been unfounded. Instead of being a lone and highly noticeable figure, he was only one of many entering and leaving the building.

Once inside, he stopped to let his stinging eyes adjust to the sudden dimness.

Gervase, Thomas sorrowed, *what evil has forced itself upon us?*

Men and women stood in a long line down the center of the *nave,* or main chamber of the church. At the front of the church, in the *chancel* which held the altar, stood a priest who briefly dipped his hands in a vessel from a stand near the altar, then touched the forehead of the person bowed below his hands.

"Move on, you bag of scum," a fat man growled at Thomas from behind. "This is no place to daydream. Not with blessings to be had."

Thomas told himself he could not spare any thoughts of grief, only thoughts of action. He fell in behind two women and slowly limped toward the front of the church.

The measured pace of the line gave Thomas time to look around. Vaulted stone ceilings gave an air of majesty and magnified the slightest noise, so that all inside only spoke in careful whispers. The nave where Thomas stood was, of course, clear of any objects except support pillars. While rumors had once reached Magnus from London that churches there actually built long bench seats called pews for the worshipers, no person bothered believing such nonsense—people had always stood to worship and *that* was the natural order of a Sabbath.

There were at least four Priests of the Holy Grail throughout the church—one in front, and three on the sides of the nave. Thomas tried to study their movements without betraying obvious interest.

Was it fear, or did he imagine they in turn studied him?

Thomas also wondered at his own lunacy. *How much trust should he have placed in Gervase? Had the blows to the old man's head addled him? What could exist beneath the altar? And how would the altar be reached—and kicked—without the notice of the four priests of the Holy Grail?*

Yet Thomas moved forward. He had no choice. Those behind him pressed heavily.

And even if he could turn away, what good would it do? There was no place to hide in Magnus, and if he bolted now, surely the watchers would then decide he had been more than a cruel-hearted beggar sent inside by Gervase to seek alms.

His heart pounded harder and harder as step by step the line advanced to the priest at the front.

Closer now, Thomas recognized him as Hugh de Gainfort. The priest, garbed in royal purple robes, dipped his hand in the liquid.

"Partake of the water of the symbol of the Grail," Hugh de Gainfort intoned, "and henceforth be loyal to the Grail itself, and to its bearers. Blessings will be sure to follow. Amen."

The woman kissed his hand. "Thank you, father."

The line moved ahead.

"Partake of the water of the symbol of the Grail," said Hugh de Gainfort without acknowledging the woman's adoration, "and henceforth be loyal to the Grail itself, and to its bearers. Blessings will be sure to follow. Amen."

The next person moved up.

Would the puppy in Thomas' arms remain quiet? Or would it draw unwanted attention?

"Partake of the water of the symbol of the Grail . . . "

Thomas wondered if the priest would hear the thumping of his heart long before he reached the front. Only ten people stood between him and Hugh de Gainfort, and Thomas could see no way to reach the altar beyond without drawing attention to himself.

What trouble had Gervase cast him into?

"and henceforth be loyal to the Grail itself, and to its bearers. Blessings will be sure to follow. Amen."

The light of the sun through the reds and blues of the stained glass windows cast soft shadows upon Hugh de Gainfort, so that if Thomas did not look closely, he would miss the hatred glittering in those eyes, hatred he had felt during their brief audience earlier in the castle keep.

Would he be recognized during the blessing? Thomas worried. *And if not, how to reach the altar? And even at the altar, what truth could there be to the old man's instructions? And even if the passage revealed itself, how could he enter unnoticed?*

Thomas swallowed in efforts to moisten his suddenly dry throat. This was madness, and he was only one step away from a blessing which . . .

"Partake of the water of the symbol of the Grail . . . " Hugh de Gainfort's hand dipped automatically into the water. Wet fingers brushed against Thomas' forehead. "and henceforth be

loyal to the Grail itself, and to its bearers. Blessings will be sure
to follow. Amen."

Thomas started to turn away. The movement drew Hugh's
eyes briefly. Suddenly those black eyes widened.

"It is you!" the priest hissed. He opened his mouth to shout.

Thomas reacted with a move he had been taught hundreds of
times by Robert of Uleran, but had never been forced to use. He
twisted his shoulders away from the priest, then spun them
back to drive forward his right hand in a shortened swing. In
that blink of an eye, Thomas managed to hit his target with his
clenched fist, middle knuckle slightly protruding. The point of
the knuckle found its target, a small bone between the ribs, just
above the priest's stomach.

The air left the priest's lungs with an audible pop. He
clutched himself and began to sway.

It happened so quickly, those behind Thomas were not sure
what they had seen.

Before Thomas could decide how best to flee, a terrifying
crash shattered the quiet whispers of the church. One of the
arched windows fell inward, burying a nearby priest. White
light from sudden sun flooded the church and danced off rising
dust.

Hugh de Gainfort dropped to his knees, still winded so badly
he could barely breathe, let alone draw enough air to shout.

Then another crash as the window farther down tumbled
inward.

The destruction—it could only be Gervase!

Thomas did not hesitate. Whatever sacrifice the old man had
just made to create the diversion must not be wasted.

All eyes were focused on the western arm of the church building, and the third window cascaded inward, as if riding the
high scream that entered with it.

Thomas darted to the altar.

What had the old man said? The panel beneath the candles, kick it sharply near the bottom. Twice.

Thomas glanced to see if Hugh de Gainfort had seen him, but the priest had sagged into a limp bundle. All others stared in horror at the sight of priceless stained glass in pieces on the stone. *If there truly was a passage, Thomas might escape without witnesses.*

Thomas kicked once. Kicked twice.

Soundlessly, the panel swung inward. It revealed a black square beneath the altar, wide enough to fit a large man.

Then another scream from outside the building. *What price had Gervase paid?*

Thomas bit his lower lip. He must ensure the sacrifice had not been made in vain. Thomas ignored the pain in his leg and sat quickly, so that his feet dangled over the edge. He pulled the puppy from beneath his arms.

"My friend, if you go to your death, so do I."

Thomas put both arms around the puppy to shield it, then let himself drop into the darkness.

1 3

Death arrived for neither.

Thomas dropped through the air for half a heartbeat. He closed his eyes and braced for the crush of impact to splatter him against the black unknown.

Then, incredibly, it felt as if arms began to wrap him tight. A great resistance began to slow his fall.

Those arms grew tighter, then brushed against his face. In the same moment, Thomas felt growing friction against his body and realized these were not the arms of a savior, but a giant sleeve of cloth, tapered into a narrowing tube.

It slowed him almost to a standstill as the tube grew so narrow that the fabric squeezed even against his face.

Then, just as it seemed he had more to fear from suffocation than from splintered bones and shredded flesh, his feet popped into open air, and he slid loose from his cloth prison.

Even though the final drop was less than the height of a chair, Thomas was not able to see the ground in time to absorb the impact; the jarring of his heels against hard ground forced loose a grunt of pain.

He recovered his breath quickly and strained to see around him.

"Wherever we are, puppy," Thomas said moments later, and glad in this darkness for the company of his whimpering friend, "let's pray it is a better alternative to what was in store for us above."

14

"**This is madness,**" Thomas whispered to the puppy. "Or do I dream a nightmare?"

Thomas reached around him to explore for walls. In the darkness, he could not even see the movement of his own arms. He pulled his eyepatch loose It did not help his vision.

Thomas forced himself to smile "Ah, puppy, you do not answer. That is a good sign. For if I were mad, or dreaming, you would speak."

The puppy whined at the gentle sadness ın the tones of those words, and squirmed in Thomas' arms as it tried to reach upward to offer comfort with well-placed licks of a tongue much too wet.

"Enough!" Thomas said through a laugh. "Next, you'll punish me by wetting yourself "

He set the puppy down

Thomas sobered immediately

So much had happened so quickly. Only yesterday, he had ruled the island castle of Magnus, and by extension, the kingdom around it. Today, he was a fugitive, marked for death or worse by the offer of a brick of gold for his head. Because of him, his friends had suffered equally. Robert of Uleran's fate was unknown, Gervase had surely died for his sacrifice of distraction, and Tiny John could only wander the streets and hope the Priests of the Holy Grail would not place any importance on his freedom.

And now?

Thomas took a deep breath to steady himself.

Now he was in pitch blackness, somewhere below Magnus in a pit or passage he had never known existed.

To return to Magnus, even if that were possible, endangered his life. Yet how long could he remain, blind, within the bowels of the earth?

A new thought struck Thomas with such force that he sucked air in sharply.

Gervase knew.

Gervase knew of the trap door below the altar.

More thoughts tumbled upon Thomas. Warnings and whispers of evil and secrets within Magnus he had heard more than once. Warnings of evil and secrets within Magnus he had tried to ignore throughout a long winter of isolation within the castle keep. Warnings of evil and secrets within Magnus that had plagued him since first conquering the kingdom.

Surely this must be part of the mystery of Magnus. Yet if Gervase knew, why had he not revealed it much earlier, before the arrival of the Priests of the Holy Grail? And if Gervase knew, but said so little, was he a friend or foe? And if Gervase were a foe, what lay ahead?

Thomas stopped his whirlwind of thoughts. No, if Gervase were foe, he would not have ensured this temporary escape

Thomas must believe. He had no choice.

He strained to remember the old man's words.

After sixty steps, you must make the leap of faith. Understand?

Make the leap of faith. You will find instructions near the burning water.

Somewhere in this darkness, he would find the answer. *But if there ever was a moment to delay the search, it was now.*

Several minutes later, a sharp yipping drew Thomas from his quiet repose.

"Puppy," he admonished in mock severeness. "Can a man not pray in peace?"

The puppy whined in relief, now that his master spoke again.

Despite the chill stillness of darkness so deep that not even fifteen minutes of adjustment had brought the faintest gray of light to his eyes, Thomas spoke in a conversational manner, as if he and the puppy were in bright sunshine, sharing the warmth of the spring day above.

"Faith is difficult to explain, puppy. But with it, prayer eases the mind much. How do I know He listens? That I cannot explain either."

A light patting reached Thomas as the puppy's tail thumped the ground to reflect contentment.

Thomas drew himself ramrod straight in the darkness as he imitated Gervase during a serious discussion. The puppy remained pressed against his feet. Thomas tucked his chin into his chest and mimicked the old man's voice. "You have a mind, Thomas. How can you remain so unwilling to learn? Religion— the organized church much as you distrust it—is the necessary structure on earth for faith in God and His promises.

"Because *some* men have twisted this structure for their own purposes is no reason to choose to cast away faith. Because the monks in your boyhood abbey showed such little faith is no reason to reflect falseness upon an essential truth."

Thomas squatted and scratched the puppy's head. He reverted to his own voice, and spoke almost absently, because his mind was already on the problems ahead. "Puppy, we are here now because of false priests making false claims upon truth."

Thomas straightened, and finished his thoughts aloud.

"There was more, of course. And should you care to listen later, it will be my delight to recount those long hours of conversation with Gervase. Because much as I did not want to believe, puppy, twice I faced death, and twice I cried to the God I did not want to believe. Explain that."

Instead of answering, the puppy shifted its weight and settled for a nap.

"Not so soon," Thomas warned his small friend. "Our journey begins."

1 5

Thomas took his first halting step with a courage which result-
ed from three things: the calm from prayer, the promise of an
explanation should he find the burning water and, strangely,
from the puppy which blundered into his legs each step he
took. A companion, no matter its size, made the eerie silence
easier to bear.

Thomas took his second step into a rough stone wall. His
groping hand prevented any injury to his face, yet Thomas recoiled as if he were struck. Any sudden contact, gentle or not,
created awesome fear in this pitch darkness.

Thomas pushed himself away, then thought against it, and
brought his right shoulder up to the wall again.

"I'll feel my way along," he told the puppy, simply as a way
to break the tension which brought sweat in rivers down his
face despite the damp chill. "It will give me warning of twists
and turns."

Thus, his fingers became his eyes.

Thomas patted the wall as he followed it, grimacing at real or imagined cobwebs. He stubbed his fingertips raw against out-crops of stone, and stumbled occasionally against objects on the ground. Twice he patted empty air—as much a fright as his original contact against stone, and each time he discovered an-other turn in the passage. He counted each step, remembering the strange message about a leap of faith. The puppy stayed with Thomas and did not complain.

Upon his sixtieth step, Thomas paused. There was nothing to indicate a leap of faith. *What had the old man meant?*

Two steps later, Thomas reached for the stone wall ahead of him and for the third time found nothing.

"Another turn," he muttered to the puppy. "Is this what the old man meant? Then why not warn me of the previous two? The shock of many more will kill me morely surely than those priests."

He slowly began to pivot right, when a low angry noise froze him.

It took a moment, but Thomas identified the echoes as growls of the puppy at his feet.

Thomas relaxed.

"Hush," he spoke downward, then moved to take his step.

The puppy growled again, with enough intensity to make the skin ripple down Thomas' back.

"Easy, my friend." Thomas knelt to hold the puppy. The growling stopped.

Thomas stood and moved again. This time the puppy bit Thomas in the foot and growled louder.

"Whelp! Have you gone crazy?"

Thomas reached down to slap the puppy for its insolence, but couldn't find it in the dark.

He groped farther, patting the ground. First behind him, then to his side, then—

Ahead! The ground ahead had disappeared.

Thomas forgot the puppy. He patted the wall on his right, found the edge of the corner and slid his hand downward, finally kneeling to reach as low as possible. *Where the corner met the ground, it was no longer a corner, but a surface which continued downward below the level of his feet.*

The skin on his back now rippled upward in fear.

"Puppy," he cried softly. A whimper answered him.

Thomas, on his knees in his blindness in the dark, crawled backward two more paces, then eased himself onto his stomach.

Now feeling safer on his belly, Thomas inched forward, feeling ahead for the edge of the drop-off with his extended right hand. He found it—as expected—and still could not escape the chill of his discovery. If he had taken that extra step. . . . Yet, perhaps if he followed the edge left, he might discover this drop-off only continued halfway across the passage. Perhaps in the dark he had only discovered a hole instead of a chasm which cut off the passage entirely.

But seconds later, he bumped into the other wall of the passage. It was indeed a chasm, all the way across!

Thomas was too spent with the jolts of fear to react with much more than a moan of despair.

"How deep?" he asked the puppy. "How far ahead to the other side?"

The answer, of course, did not arrive.

Thomas crawled ahead as far as he dared. With his dangling hand, he reached down into the blackness. *After all, perhaps this drop is a mere foot or two,* he thought. *I could be stuck here forever, afraid to step downward.*

Thomas slumped. His exploring hand had found nothing. Even after drawing his sword and extending it to reach farther, he could not prove to himself that the drop was only a shallow ditch.

Long minutes later, he raised his head from the ground again.

He knew he had three choices. *Leap ahead and trust the chasm was narrow enough to cross. Drop into the chasm and trust its bottom was just beyond his reach. Or retrace his steps.*

He chose to reverse direction.

Sixty-two counted steps and two turns later, he was back to his starting point. Thomas looked upward, half expecting to see light where the priests might be peering downward from the trapdoor beneath the altar. But he knew that would not be. No one had seen his escape. And now he was trapped here. Unless the other direction yielded better results.

Now, however, he patted the ground and crawled ahead. Since he had passed his original beginning point, he did not know whether he should expect another sudden chasm ahead in the opposite direction.

Thomas did not travel far.

The wall turned sharply, then sharply again.

By now, as blind as if both eyes had been covered with patches, Thomas was accustomed to thinking with the feel of his fingers. He knew he had reached the end of the passage and was now proceeding in his original direction, except along the left wall.

"Are you with me puppy?" Thomas called, although he did not need ask. He only wanted to be reassured by a familiar noise in the blackness.

The puppy sounded a low whine and Thomas smiled through his misery. He had no choice but to proceed sixty-two steps back to the chasm and from there, debate his bleak prospects in this silence that now seemed louder than any noise he had ever faced.

Unless . . .

Unless the passage split! After all, he had only traced the right-hand side of it. Perhaps the left-hand side broke into another passage and all he need do was find it by patiently continuing the blind groping.

Thomas called the puppy closer and tried to find its ears in the darkness. The puppy found his hand first, and gently licked Thomas' fingers.

It was then Thomas realized the rawness had become broken skin and the puppy was trying to lick away blood. In his fears, Thomas had not noticed the damage done by the walls to his fingers.

He took a deep breath and moved ahead. Yes, the left wall must split into a new passage somewhere before the chasm. *It must.*

It did not.

Sixty-two steps and two turns later, Thomas was again on his belly, feeling ahead in the terrifying darkness for that drop-off.

He found it, retreated slightly, and banged the ground in frustration, uncaring of the new pain.

How could he possibly overcome this barrier?

Then a tiny flicker caught his eye.

Thomas almost missed it, so much had he given up on using vision to aid his senses.

He blinked, then squinted.

Five minutes passed.

Another minute. *There!* The flicker again. It brightened, then dropped to nothing. Thomas strained to focus and pinpoint its location. Ten agonizing minutes later, another flare, hardly more than a candle suddenly snuffed.

It dawned slowly upon Thomas.

Burning water.

He was seeing the light of a far-off flame, light he had missed the first time here because it flared so rarely and softly, light which reflected and bounced through one or two more turns of the passageway.

1 6

Thomas lowered himself and sat, knees huddled against his chest. The puppy leaned against him, whining occasionally, growling for no apparent reason in other moments.

A phrase echoed through his head. *Understand? Make the leap of faith.*

Why had the old man been so urgent with those five words? Why had he repeated those words and repeated no other part of his instructions?

Make the leap of faith.

It reminded him of a part of a conversation once held with Gervase. To pass time, Thomas spoke aloud to the puppy.

"During the quiet of an early morning," Thomas said, "Gervase told me this. No matter how much you learn or debate the existence of God, no matter how much you apply your mind to Him, you cannot satisfy your soul."

The puppy rested his chin on Thomas' upper thigh.

"The old man said there must come a time at the beginning **of** your faith when you let go and simply trust, a time when you must make the leap of faith, something much like a. . . . " Thomas faltered as he suddenly realized the significance of Gervase's repeated words.

He finished the thought silently. *Something much like a leap into the darkness.*

That entire conversation flooded Thomas' mind. They had talked often, usually in the early hours, after Thomas had walked the ramparts of Magnus. This conversation had taken place barely a month after Thomas had conquered Magnus. Gervase had talked simply of faith in answer to all of Thomas' questions.

It is a leap into the darkness, Thomas, he had said. *God awaits you on the other side. First your heart finds Him, then your mind will understand Him more clearly so that all evidence points toward the unshakable conclusion you could not find before. After that leap your faith will grow stronger with time. But faith, any faith, is trust and that small leap into darkness.*

"No, Gervase," Thomas said aloud. "I cannot do this. You ask too much."

Damp chill settled on Thomas.

Make the leap of faith. Understand? Sixty steps and make the leap of faith. Thomas had no doubt now that Gervase had meant he should do the same now.

Yet how could Thomas blindly jump ahead? What lay on the other side? What lay below?

An encouraging thought struck him.

Magnus was surrounded by lake waters. Indeed, the wells of Magnus had very little distance to go before reaching water. And this passage was already below the surface. How far down, then, before reaching water from this passageway?

Might he drop his sword to test the depth of the chasm?

Make the leap of faith.

No, he could not venture weaponless.

Might he drop the puppy ahead to test the depth of the chasm? Or cast the puppy ahead to test the width?

Make the leap of faith.

No, not when the creature had first warned him of the chasm. Not when the creature trusted him so.

Make the leap of faith.

Thomas frowned. Had he not regarded Gervase with equal trust? And if Thomas now showed such concern for the puppy, would not Gervase show that much more concern for Thomas?

Make the leap of faith.

Thomas finally allowed himself to decide what he had known since recalling the old man's words about faith.

He must leap into the darkness

Ten times Thomas paced large steps backward from the edge of the chasm. Ten times he repaced them forward again, careful to reach down and ahead with his sword on the eighth, ninth, and tenth steps to establish he had not yet reached the edge.

"Puppy," he said as he retraced his steps backward yet again, "if leap we must, I shall not do it from a standstill. Faith or not, I doubt our God or Gervase enjoys stupidity"

Thomas had debated briefly whether to take the puppy. But only briefly. The extra weight was slight, and he could not bear to make it across safely and hear forever in his mind abandoned whimpers of a puppy left for death

Thomas squatted and felt for the line he had gouged into the ground to mark the ten paces away from the edge

He rehearsed the planned action in his mind. He would sprint only eight steps—for he could not trust running paces to be as small as his ten carefully stretched and marked paces. On the eighth step, he would leap and dive and release the puppy. His hands would give him first warning of impact—he prayed for that impact—and at best he might knock loose his breath. The puppy would travel slightly farther, and at best, tumble and roll.

At worst, neither would reach the other side of that unknown chasm in this terrible blackness.

Thomas drew a deep breath. He hugged the puppy once, then tucked it into the crook of his right arm.

Make the leap of faith.

"God be with us," he whispered. Then plunged ahead.

1 7

At full sprint, Thomas drove upward on the eighth step and left the ground.

In the black around him, he had no way to measure the height he reached, no way to measure how far forward he flew, and no way to measure how much he dropped.

It seemed to take forever, the rush of air in his ears, the half sob of fear escaping his throat, and the squirm of the puppy in his outstretched hands.

The puppy!

In midair, Thomas pushed him ahead and released him from his hands. Before he could even think of praying for safety, or the safety of the puppy, the heels of his hands hit solid ground, and he bumped and skidded onto his nose, then chin, then, as his head bounced upward, onto his chest and stomach.

Time, with him, skidded back to normal, and Thomas could count his heartbeats thudding in his ears.

Was he across? Or at the bottom of a shallow ditch?

The puppy's confused whimper sounded nearby.

Thomas coughed and rolled to his feet.

"My friend," he said, "we seem to be alive. But across?"

Thomas answered his own question by turning around and crawling back. Moments later, his hands found an edge!

Thomas grinned in the darkness.

The next two turns in the passageway and the next eighty-eight steps took nearly an hour. Although the occasional flare of reflected light grew stronger and stronger, it provided little illumination, and Thomas dared not to risk another unseen chasm.

He reached that final turn.

His reward was another flicker of light. This time, the flame itself—n0t a reflection—straight ahead and far down the passageway.

As Thomas walked closer, the rising and falling light provided him more clues about the passage.

The walls were shored with large square blocks of stone, unevenly placed. He understood immediately why his groping fingers had received such punishment in the total darkness behind him.

The passage was hardly higher than his head, and wide enough to fit three men walking abreast.

Other than that, nothing. No clues to the builders. No clues to its reason for existence. No clues to its age.

Thomas half ran the final few steps to the light. The leg he had managed to forget in the previous few hours ached again with the extra movement, but he did not mind.

Gervase had promised the knowledge he needed. It could only mean a message. And if Gervase had managed to leave the message, Gervase had managed to escape again.

Thomas noted the source of the light. It was imbedded in the wall, as if a hand had scooped away part of the stone. A wick of cloth rose above a clear liquid, and from it came the solitary tongue of flame.

Burning water!

He did not examine the light long, because the puppy whined and sniffed at a leather sack barely visible in the shadows along the wall below the flame. Thomas pulled the sack away before the puppy could bury its nose in it entirely.

He understood the puppy's anxiousness as soon as he opened it.

Cheese. Bread. And cooked chicken legs. All wrapped in clean cloth.

Thank you, Gervase. Sudden moisture filled Thomas' mouth as he realized how hungry he was. With his teeth, he ripped into a fat chicken leg, chewed a mouthful, then tore pieces free with his fingers to drop to the puppy.

More objects remained in the bag.

Thomas pulled free a large candle. He dipped the end into the flame in the wall and immediately doubled his light. Next from the bag came a candle holder, hooded so the bearer could walk and shed light without fear of killing the flame.

Finally, Thomas pulled free a scrolled parchment, tied shut with a delicate ribbon.

He wiped his hands of chicken grease, set the candle holder on the ground and sat beside it.

The puppy nosed his palms for more food.

"Later," Thomas said absently. His fingers, no longer bleeding and suddenly without pain as he focused on the parchment, trembled as he pulled the ribbon loose and unscrolled the parchment.

The ink lettering bold and well spaced, as if the writer guessed Thomas might be forced to read the parchment in dim light.

Thomas, if you read this, it is only because, as I feared, the
Druids, disguised as Priests of the Holy Grail, have imprisoned you in your own dungeon. Yet, if you read this, it is
because you dared make the leap of faith I requested, and
in so doing have proved you are not a Druid.

Druids! The shock was as of an arrow piercing his heart. Then
Thomas rubbed his forehead in puzzlement. *Imprisoned in my
own dungeon—I did not arrive here from the dungeon. And to suggest
I might be a Druid—how could Gervase even dare to think the un-
thinkable? I have spent the entire winter in fear of their return.*

Yes, my friend, the chasm you leaped was a test. Were you
one of the Druids, you would have known that these passages and halls—

Passages and halls? Thomas sighed. This message created more
mystery than it solved. Did Gervase imply that all of Magnus
was riddled with secret tunnels?

—passages and halls are buried so deep in the island that
anything more than several feet below their level would
fill with water. You, as a Druid, would already be familiar
with this. You, as a Druid, would have confidently
stepped down and walked across, even without light to
guide you.

That you are reading this means you are not a Druid, for
in that shallow, dry moat, I had placed a dozen adders.

Adders! Snakes with venom so potent that only a scratch of
poison could kill. *A dozen adders!* In the darkness, the puppy had
not growled at the drop-off, but at what his nose had

warned him of.

Thomas scratched the puppy behind the ears, and shuddered at what might have happened had Gervase not urged him to make the leap of faith.

Thus, you now have my trust, Thomas. I regret I could not give it earlier. There is much to tell you, my friend, and I fear by the time you return to Magnus, I will not be alive to be the one who reveals to you the epic struggle between the Druids and Merlins.

Merlin! Here was mention again of the ancient days of King Arthur. For Merlin, King Arthur's adviser, had become a legend equalling the king himself!

I cannot say much in this letter, for who is to guess what others may stumble across it should you not take the leap of faith and be the first to arrive here. Let me simply ask you to consider the books of your childhood. It was not chance that they were placed near you, those books of ancient knowledge from faraway lands. It was not chance that one of us was there to raise you, to teach you, to guide you, to urge you to reconquer Magnus, to show you the way. It was not chance that I spread the legend of the rescuing angel shortly before your birth.

These new words were not the piercing of an arrow, but now the bludgeoning of a club. *Gervase knew of those precious books hidden near the abbey? Impossible!* At the significance of the message, Thomas could hardly breathe. He remembered too the night he had conquered Magnus on wings of an angel, how the entire population of Magnus had gathered enough strength from his arrival to overthrow its evil lord, simply because of a legend which all believed. *This had been planned before Thomas was born?*

Yet none of this knowledge could I share, Thomas, much as I treasured our conversations. For too many years passed with you alone in the abbey. We did not know if they had discovered you and converted you. We did not know if you were one of them, allowed to conquer in appearance only, so that we might reveal the final secrets of Magnus to you, secrets so important I cannot even hint of them now.

You trusted me to arrive here, I beg of you to continue that trust. Your destiny has grown even more crucial—we did not expect the Druids to act so boldly, so soon. Even now, perhaps they have the power to conquer completely. You, as a born Merlin, must stop them.

Thomas wanted to protest aloud. *A born Merlin. I am a born Merlin? Gervase, how can you reveal so much, yet reveal so little?*

Follow this passage, Thomas. It will take you to safety. Return to the abbey of your childhood. Search for the answers among your books. Trust no person. Our stakes are too high. The Druids must not prevail.

19

KATHERINE
In Paris

SPRING A. D. 1313

Katherine looked up, startled, as a shadow crossed the pages of her open book.

"I'm sorry, my child," a soft voice reassured her. "The thoughts I interrupted, they must have been enjoyable. Your face showed such pleasure. And I was clumsy to. . . . "

She blushed. "Frere Dominique, it is I who should apologize for daydreaming. The progress I have made with this Latin has not been remarkable. With all due respect to the author, it is . . . it is. . . . "

Katherine fumbled for a tactful way to express how boring she found 11th-century German philosophy. Her French failed her, however, and all she could do was shrug and look down modestly.

"Katherine," Frere Dominique admonished. "Is it not enough you have won an old priest's heart? And now you take advantage of it with beautiful helplessness that is merely acted?"

Katherine laughed. Little escaped the old priest. He moved with an energy of a far younger man. Although he was plump and graying and always wore the smile of a jolly man, his eyes gleamed sharp in unguarded moments—or during the rough and tumble arguments in logic he and Katherine had enjoyed to pass time throughout the long winter.

The priest smiled indulgently. How peaceful it was here in the library of the royal palace. On days like this—with the sun casting golden warmth through opened windows, with the quiet of the large room broken only by far-off shouts of laughter and closer by, the birds in the royal garden—Frere Dominique's thoughts often strayed to heaven.

Yes, he would tell himself as he did now, heaven shall be the peace of precious books arranged in order and the solitude of one free to seek more and more knowledge, always aware of Him the highest, and—Frere Dominique sighed because of the news he must deliver and how he would miss Katherine—with angels of sweetness such as this one nearby.

Frere Dominique studied Katherine's face. These might be their final moments together. He would miss the joy of admiring her fine, high cheekbones, the curve of her smile, the depth and innocence of her gaze.

"Yes, Father?" Katherine asked his searching eyes. "Is something wrong?"

Frere Dominique nodded. "Only for me," he said. "You see, when I tell you my heart has been stolen, it is not merely the flattery of a man who enjoys too much—" the priest patted his stomach "—your touch with our French recipes. I shall truly miss your presence here."

Katherine stood quickly. She took one of the priest's hands in hers, and squeezed it tight. "He has returned?"

Frere Domique nodded, then shook his head mournfully. "After an absence of six months, he refuses to accept the hospitality of one night's stay here. Even now, that old scoundrel is in the stable, preparing a horse for you."

Katherine dropped the priest's warm hand. "Travel? So soon? Did he mention. . . ?"

Once again, Katherine blushed.

"England?" Frere Dominique finished for her.

Katherine nodded, watched the priest's face and waited.

"Yes," Frere Dominique finally said. Then smiled at her un-concealed expression. "Your face again carries the look I inter-rupted moments ago. Who is he that captures your thoughts, Katherine? Were I three decades younger, I would be smitten with jealousy."

Katherine and the old man rode for two days to reach the harbor town of Dieppe on the French side of the English Channel.

She knew the old man was anxious. He did not question the price offered for the horses in Dieppe, although it was scandal-ously low. And half an hour later, he did not barter with the ship's captain for passage across the Channel.

Three days of pitched and gray North Sea brought them to cliffs of Scarborough. Once again, the old man did not waste time searching for the fairest price of horseflesh, and paid dou-ble what he should have.

They rode 30 miles, directly to an obscure abbey north and east of the town of York, stopping only when the sun went down.

18

"**Patience**," the old man said, "is well known as a virtue."

"Then I shall be nominated for sainthood," Katherine replied. "For nearly a week now, I have waited for you to inform me of the reason for our madness of haste."

She waved at the land around them. "And now you ask me to sit here for hours, perhaps days, on the mere chance that Thomas might arrive in this remote valley."

"Keep your hands still," the old man admonished. "He must have no hint of our presence."

"He will not arrive."

The old man chuckled. "Your voice betrays your hope."

To that, Katherine did not reply. For the old man spoke truth.

His earlier promise—and only information—had been that Thomas would arrive. And the old man had never been wrong, at least not in her memory

So they had settled into the side of a hill barely a half hour earlier, just as the morning sun rose to show her that the valley below was narrow and compressed, with more rock and stunted trees on the slopes than sweet grass and sheep.

Although they were near the exposed summit of the valley, the old man had shrewdly chosen a vantage point among the shadows of large rocks.

Lower down, trees guarded the tiny river which wound past the abbey a half-mile downstream.

The old man had pointed at a jumble of rocks and boulders on the river, some as large as a peasant's hut. "There," he had said, "is hidden a dry, cool cave, invisible except to those who have been led to its narrow entrance among the granite and growing bush. There is his destination."

And now, long enough later so that the prickling of the sun's first heat had brought forth the ants which marched in the dust in front of her, Katherine brought the discussion back to the questions she wanted answered.

"Not only shall I receive a sainthood for patience, but if ignorance is bliss, I shall be the happiest saint to have walked this earth."

Her comment drew another chuckle.

"Yes," the old man said. "I tell you little. But for your own protection."

"No," Katherine corrected. "For the protection of Magnus."

She then repeated oft heard words. "After all, I cannot divulge what I do not know."

That drew a sigh.

"Katherine," he said, "not even I know the entire plan. We all have our tasks, and must trust to the whole."

Would it be fair, she wondered, *to push him now for more?*

She hesitated. *Was it fair*, she countered herself, *to know so little?*

So she decided to ask, almost with dread at his anticipated anger. "Yes," she said softly. "There is truth in that. You fear that I might be taken by the Druids and be forced to betray us.

But if something should happen to you? How could I carry on our battle without more knowledge than I have now?"

The old man dropped his head. Instead of anger, sadness filled his voice. "There is truth in that. And I've wondered how long it would take for you to use my sword of defense upon myself."

She waited, sensing victory, but feeling no enjoyment in it.

He continued. "In the cave below are books. In Latin, French, even Italian. But mostly Latin. Once, as you know, those of us in Magnus had the leisure to translate from all languages into that universal word."

"Books?" Katherine was incredulous. "Here in this valley. But that is treasure beyond value! Why here?"

"Indeed," he said. "Treasure beyond value. More than you know. These are not books coveted by the wealthy for beauty and worth. In that cave lies knowledge brought from lands as far away as the eastern edge of the world. All for Thomas to use in his solitary battle."

"That is why you are so certain he will return," Katherine breathed.

"The message told me Magnus has fallen. With no money and no army, he has no choice but to seek power from the knowledge in that cave."

"Much as he did to first conquer Magnus," Katherine said absently.

A sharp intake of breath from the old man. "You know that?"

"Wings of an angel," she said simply. "How else could he have had such a secret?"

"Of course," he said. "You would not fail to see the obvious."

Should she feel guilty? She had not lied, but she had not told the old man that Thomas had once hinted to her of these books. And that he had regretted it later as he banished her from Magnus.

Katherine now realized the immensity of the secret Thomas had held, not knowing she was one of his watchers. But her new information only led to more questions.

"How did the books arrive here? When? Why?"

"The books arrived by horse. Along the path of the Crusades. And that is all I wish to say."

There was a finality to his tone that told her not to pursue those questions farther. So Katherine puzzled through more thoughts, then changed the direction of her query. "Why must we continue to watch? Surely he now needs our help."

The old man shook his head. "Not until we are certain to which side he belongs. Our only word was that Magnus has fallen. Nothing else arrived from Gervase to guide us farther. In this game of masks behind masks, we can only wait."

Katherine finished for the old man. It was a familiar argument. "For if he were a Druid, he would act as if he were not. Now, perhaps, it was convenient for them to assume open control of Magnus. And equally convenient for them to send him forth as bait."

He in turn finished her oft used argument. "Yet if he is not one of them, we can do so much good by revealing ourselves. Together, our fight will be stronger."

They both sighed. It was an argument with no answer to trust. Too much depended on Thomas.

When he arrived, they almost missed him.

Years of avoiding the nearby harsh monks in his boyhood had taught Thomas every secret deer path in the surrounding hills. At times, he would approach a seemingly solid stand of brush, then slip sideways into an invisible opening among the jagged branches and later reappear quietly farther down the hill.

His familiarity with the terrain, however, did not make him less cautious.

It was only the loud caws of a disgruntled crow which warned Katherine and the old man. Even then, it took them twenty minutes to see his slow movement.

From above, they saw Thomas circle the jumbled rocks near the river once. Then he slipped into a nearby crevice and surveyed the area.

"He was trained well," the old man whispered approval. "He has no reason to be suspicious, yet still he remains disciplined."

Minute after minute passed.

"He counts to one thousand," the old man explained. "He was taught that this cave was the most important secret of all. Taught never to let anyone discover the entrance."

Thomas circled slowly once more, sometimes visible, sometimes not.

Katherine ached to see his face close. To see if looking into his eyes would stir remembered feelings. But she too had been taught discipline, and held herself motionless, with nothing of those thoughts crossing her face.

Then she noticed something.

"He walks awkwardly," she whispered. "Not from the bag he carries. But as if hunched."

Then she gasped as that hump on his back moved. And just before Thomas disappeared into the cave, she received a glimpse of his burden as it poked its nose out from the back of his shirt.

"A puppy," she said in amazement. "An entire kingdom rides on his shoulders, and in its place he carries a puppy."

20

Two days passed.

Yet during the long hours of waiting, Katherine could satisfy little more of her curiosity through discussion. The old man insisted on near perfect silence. He also insisted on alternating watch duty. One must sleep while the other observed the rocks of the entrance.

The few moments they shared awake were spent sharing the sack of breads and cheeses they had carried with them.

At night, they moved closer down to the rocks of the river and settled into a nearby crevice in the hill. They could not trust the light of the moon to remain unclouded, and Thomas might leave at any hour. Twice already he had alarmed them with sudden appearances, only to fill a leather bag with water and return to the cave.

At night then, the old man had whispered to Katherine, their ears must serve as their eyes, for if they failed to follow Thomas to his next destination, the plan would surely be doomed.

Tell me more of the plan, Katherine had wanted to ask, but did not. She knew her duty, and what the old man knew of the plan would only be revealed when he deemed it proper.

So she sat, shivering in the early hours of the third day. Despite her coldness, the discipline she had been taught since birth did not leave her. She did not let the shivers shake her body; she resembled so closely in motion the rock around her that once a fox almost blundered across her feet. At the last moment, it caught her scent and leapt sideways to disappear into the dark jumble of trees and rocks.

That was the only break in the monotony. Yet, except for the shivering, Katherine did not mind. In these quiet moments, she felt at peace.

Soon, the rhythms of approaching day would begin, telling her that God's order still remained in nature, even among the confusion of the affairs of men and their struggles which had brought her to this quiet valley. Faint gray would brush the horizon first. Then tentative and sporadic chirps of faraway birds, as if each hardly believed it was to be given the gift of another new day. The rustling of the small night creatures would stop in response.

Each minute of growing light would bring her unexpected pleasures. Yesterday, it had been the careful and delicate stepping of a spider across large beads of dew on its web, across a branch so close to Katherine's face that she could see each drop of water bend, but not quite break, with the weight of the spider. The day before, she'd seen a rabbit, trailed by six tiny bundles of fur, each intent on tumbling exactly in the mother rabbit's footsteps.

Part of Katherine knew that she chose to focus on the hill around her because she wanted relief from the questions she could not yet ask the old man.

She knew his urgency stemmed from those reports that Magnus had once again fallen, and with that, at least, she understood the need for action. *Without Magnus . . .* she had been taught the history and tradition of the Merlins and hardly dared contemplate how many centuries of careful guidance were on the brink of destruction.

But why the importance of Thomas?

Deep as her feelings for him might run, warm as the skin on her face might flush as she remembered him, Katherine *could* force herself to remain objective enough to wonder why so much rested upon his shoulders.

Where were the other Merlins of this generation? Must Thomas combat the Druids alone and unknowing of battles which had been fought for centuries?

And why now the extreme urgency? After all, until Thomas had recaptured the kingdom the previous summer, Magnus had been under the control of Druids for twenty years. Surely the passing of a month, two months, could not determine the battle now?

Surely —

"Katherine."

She turned her head slightly to acknowledge she had heard the old man's waking words.

"Day is nearly upon us."

So it was. Despite her determination to contemplate the beauty of creation, those faint licks of gray had been banished by pale blue while her thoughts had wandered.

Katherine stirred, ready to pick her careful way back to the observation point farther back.

"Wait!"

She froze. And immediately understood.

Below her, Thomas had finally moved out of the cave and into sight. Without the sack of food he had carried inside. With the leather bag for water. Without the puppy.

He wore the plain brown garb of a simple monk.

They followed him along an isolated path in the forest south

of the small Harland Moor abbey. Katherine and the old man did not follow Thomas together. Rather, the old man remained ahead. It was his duty to melt invisibly into the trees and keep Thomas in sight. Katherine, a hundred yards behind and less adept at stealth, simply kept the old man in her line of vision.

At times, she lost sight of him completely. She marveled again and again at how silently he flitted from tree to tree, bush to bush.

An hour later, the old man held up a hand of warning, then settled unseen into a crouch.

Katherine responded by doing the same.

Five minutes later, the old man was up again, and moving ahead. This strung out march of three, Thomas unaware and in the lead, continued for another half hour until they reached the road leading into the town of Helmsley.

The old man waited for her at the side of the road.

"He is ahead of us, of course," he told Katherine. "I have no doubt he is going to town. Much as we needed to stop there before going to the valley."

Katherine raised an eyebrow in question. "His detour?"

"Gold," the old man replied. "He has retrieved some of the gold he had buried before leaving here with the knight for Magnus last summer. The gold he had earned from the gallows in Helmsley. And gold can only mean he has purchases in mind."

The old man's prediction proved correct.

They next saw Thomas near the Helmsley stables where they had left their own horses a few days earlier. Watching discreetly proved to be no problem. Not with the usual crowds around the market stalls.

Thomas engaged himself in conversation with the ruddy-faced fat man who tended the stables.

After five minutes, both nodded. The fat man disappeared inside the stable and returned with a middle-sized gray horse.

Thomas shook his head. The fat man shrugged. Another five minutes of conversation, this time with much animated movement of hands by both.

The fat man again entered the stable. This time he returned with a large roan stallion. Even from their vantage point, Katherine could appreciate the power suggested by the muscles that rippled and flinched as the horse occasionally shook itself of flies.

A few more minutes of conversation. A snort of derisive laughter from the fat man reached them. And yet again, he entered the stables. He brought out not a horse, but shabby blankets and saddlebags customarily placed on donkeys.

Thomas nodded and the fat man departed. Instead of swinging onto the horse, Thomas threw a blanket over it, and cinched on the saddlebags. He remained on foot, and led the horse away by its halter.

As soon as he was safely out of sight, Katherine and the old man approached the stable man.

The old man flashed a bronze coin.

The stable man grunted recognition. "The two of you." He looked at the coin and sneered. "I thought you'd both died. I've kept both your mounts in oats for three days. You expect that to pay the fare?"

"No," the old man said. He pulled a tiny gold coin from deep within his cloak and handed that to the stable man. The fat man bit the coin to test for softness, then said, "It's barely enough, but I'm not one to take advantage of strangers."

"It's a third more than you expected," the old man said quietly. He then showed the bronze coin again. "And this is yours if you tell us what the little sparrow heard."

"Eh?"

The old man fluttered his hand skyward. "The little sparrow flitting around as you spoke to that monk's assistant. What harm could there be in telling us words from a sparrow's mouth?"

The fat man leered comprehension. "Ah, that sparrow. Now I recall." He leaned forward and widened his leer to show dark stumps for teeth. "Unfortunately, that sparrow's a shy one."

A second bronze coin appeared in front of the stable man.

"He told me he wanted a horse that could outrun any in York. That was all."

"You spent ten minutes in conversation," Katherine protested.

The stable man looked at her darkly, then back at the old man. "It's a sad day when a woman child interrupts business of grown men."

Katherine rose on her toes to answer, but caught the slight warning wave of the old man's hand.

"I'll see she learns her lesson," the old man said. He then stroked his chin. "York? Hasn't its earl fallen from power?"

"It's what I said too," the stable man nodded. "I told him what even the deaf and blind know. The Earl of York now rots in his own dungeon."

The fat man paused.

"Yes?" the old man prompted.

"It's peculiar. When I said that, the assistant told me that's exactly why he needed the horse."

2 1

Katherine knew the old man had no appreciation for foolishness, so she waited an hour to ask her question. By then, they had traveled five miles along the road to York. By then, she had sifted through enough of her thoughts to know which question to ask. Even if she would not start with it.

"We have not reached nor passed Thomas yet," she began. "This means one of two things."

"Yes?" the old man asked in good humor. It always lifted his spirits when Katherine applied her training.

"He either mounted his horse as soon as he was out of sight of the town, and has ridden it fast enough to keep the distance between us. Or—"

"How do you know it will be the second and not the first?" the old man interrupted.

Katherine smiled. "Because he wants to appear as a lowly monk's assistant leading a master's horse from one town to the next. He doesn't dare ride, because too many travel this road, and many would wonder at someone dressed so poorly, mounted on such a fine horse."

The old man clapped approval. "So he has . . ."

"Thomas has undoubtedly returned to the abbey to retrieve what he needs from the cave, to fill those saddlebags." Katherine paused at the thought and what it meant. "He is arming himself."

"Yes, my friend." The old man said nothing more, and they passed the next hundred yards with only the clopping of the horses' hooves to break their companionable silence. A breeze at their backs kept the dust from rising, and Katherine let it lull her thoughts away from her question.

She turned her gaze downward as the minutes passed. Not for the first time did Katherine stare at the road and wonder at the Roman soldiers who had set these stones more than a thousand years earlier, even before the time of Merlin himself. York had been an outpost in the wild interior—the old man had explained five days previously as they had departed Scarborough—while Scarborough itself forty miles east had been the coastal watchpost. From the high cliffs of Scarborough, the Roman sentries could easily spot enemy ships, and the efficient road to the interior made it easy to shuffle legions of soldiers back and forth between Scarborough and York. And now, hundreds of years later, it carried the everyday traffic between the towns along that route.

"Katherine."

She pulled away from her thoughts

"What question do you have?"

"You can read me that well?" Katherine said.

"You had no need to impress me with your guesses. Except that I am sometimes impatient with meaningless prattle, and it seemed as if you sought to discuss Thomas more."

Katherine felt her face color as she noticed the old man's tiny grin of comprehension and the twinkle in the old man's eyes

He knew too well her thoughts of Thomas.

She also knew the old man did not like false modesty or coy games, so she simply asked her question with no further hesitation.

"Why York?" she blurted. "Thomas knows—as do all—that the Priests of the Holy Grail rule it as surely as they rule Magnus. Moreover, the Earl of York, in chains or not, is a sworn enemy of Thomas. Why enter the lion's den?"

The old man spoke so softly she could barely hear. "I've wondered that myself. Perhaps he has decided if he frees the Earl of York, they will swear a pact of allegiance, and together fight the Priests. Perhaps he simply wishes to observe the Priests without fear of recognition by the townspeople as would happen to him in Magnus. After all, he knows, as do you, the first maxim of warfare is simple. 'Know thine enemy.' "

Another hundred yards.

The riders swayed to the rhythm of the slow plodding. With less urgency now than during their previous travels, there seemed little purpose in taxing the horses.

The leaves of the oak trees lining the road had already burst from buds. Dappled shade covered them as they moved steadily along the road. Soon, the leaves would be full, and the road would be entirely covered from the sun.

Had only four seasons passed since Thomas first entered Magnus? Only four seasons since she had first spoken to him in a candlemaker's shop? Only four seasons since his long-predicted arrival had captured her heart?

Another thought haunted her. *In another four seasons, would Thomas still be alive and the battle continuing?*

"Your face is an open book, my friend." The gentle voice once again took her from her thoughts.

"Even if Thomas frees the earl," Katherine blurted, "or if Thomas knows the Priests of the Holy Grail as well as they know themselves, how can he prevail against their miracles? Blood of the martyr. The weeping statue." Katherine resisted the urge to cross herself as peasants did to speak of such sacred things.

"The blood and statue I can explain easily," the old man said shortly after. "How he is to prevail, I cannot."

"Please," Katherine said quietly. "I have great curiosity. The blood of the martyr. The weeping statue."

"Simple," the old man said. "The blood is nothing holier than a mixture of chalk and the water from rusted iron, sprinkled with salt water."

He snorted. "Those false priests pray for the congealed blood to turn to liquid, but they help their prayers by gently shaking the vial. That's all it takes. And when it settles, it appears like thickly clotted blood."

"And the weeping statue?"

Another snort. "Those stone eyes only weep water when brought from the warmth into the coolness of the church. More sham and trickery."

"We too could duplicate those miracles?"

"And prey upon ignorant superstition? Never. And we chose to always remain hidden from the people."

"Thomas could expose those tricks for what they are!" Katherine said. "Surely if enough see the truth, the Priests would be known as frauds and lose their power to rule."

"No, Katherine. There is only one Thomas, and thousands upon thousands to convince, even if he could. People treasure their misconceptions, cling to them and never look beyond. Besides, how long could Thomas travel as a free man during his demonstrations against the Priests?"

Katherine puzzled for several moments. "An army, then. Thomas will observe the Priests, discover their weaknesses, and muster an army to strike as he sees best."

The old man shook his head. "With what money might he raise an army? With what allegiances? Moreover, the Priests now maintain rule because all believe they are the spokesmen for God. What man, what knight dares raise a sword against the Almighty with false miracles plain to see and so eagerly believed?"

They traveled much farther before Katherine spoke again. "There seems to be little hope for him. For us."

The old man snorted. "Perhaps Thomas is not meant to prevail. I repeat, we still have no certainty to which side he belongs. They must know he is watched by us, even if they do not know the watchers. An apparent defeat of Thomas will lead us to trust him, and with trust, we might impart to him the final secrets they need so badly."

Katherine could only set her chin stubbornly as a means to hold back a sigh of sadness.

The never-ending logic of argument.

She closed her eyes and spoke to the sky. "This waiting is a cruel game."

2 2

Their long wait the next morning at the massive gates to the town wall was rewarded as the bells rang *sext* to mark *midday*.

Unlike Magnus, the walls around the entire town of York did not have the advantage of a protecting lake. Because of that, they were much thicker to better protect against battering rams. Indeed, so wide were these walls that atop were large chambers built from equally massive stone blocks.

Katherine and the old man were close to the west gate of York. Almost directly above them and built into the high arch above the entrance to the town, was one of the prisons of York.

An open window had been cut into each of the four walls of the prison, hardly large enough for a small boy to crawl through. Despite that restriction, and despite the sheer thirty-foot drop to the ground, iron bars had been placed into the windows as a final barrier to prisoners with dreams of escape.

When Katherine looked up, she imagined the occasional dark shadow of movement through the window closest to her. She did not look up often, however. Embedded into the stone walls were iron pikes. Upon three, the heads of three men were impaled, staring their silent horror upon the town as warning to those who might also become rebels.

Mostly, then, Katherine watched a stream of peasants and craftsmen enter town beneath those gateway arch prisons. The air was noisy with shouts and curses at stubborn donkeys, the cackles of geese, the grunts of pigs.

This steady stream disappeared quickly once inside York as the cobbled road twisted and turned its way inside to dozens of side streets. Some strangers—those new to the wonders of York —stopped almost immediately at one of the shops on the side of the road. Others—the more experienced and unwilling to be fleeced immediately—continued for the markets.

They stood among the jostling people bartering for the wares of the cook shop positioned to sell to the impatiently hungry. The aromas of the food did not make their waiting easy. Katherine could smell roasted joints and meat pasties—all at a price double what one could expect to pay closer to the town center.

To amuse herself as she waited—for they had taken their spot the previous afternoon, abandoned it with reluctance at sunset when the gate closed, and resumed it at dawn—Katherine tested her powers of observation by scanning the crowd for pickpockets.

She saw two. One particularly clever pickpocket played the role of a drunk. He staggered and bounced into people, enduring their abuse and leaving with the coins he had dipped during the confusion of the impact of his fall against them.

Katherine hoped the jugglers would return. Yesterday, a half hour had passed in the space of a drawn breath, so adept were these men with tossed and whirling swords and flames. Even the old man beside her had coughed admiration and thrown small coins in their direction.

Or perhaps the man with the wrestling bear would entertain again. What a treat that had been. Of course, she told herself, sights like this were to be expected in York. After all, with its ten thousand inhabitants, only London exceeded it in size.

Katherine lapsed into her favorite daydream, the one where she was able to explain as much as she knew to Thomas. She formed an image of his face and tried not to hear his last words to her as he banished her from Magnus. She tried to picture his smile as he finally understood why she had withheld the truth.

The old man nudged her just as the last of the sext bells rang. "He approaches," came his whisper. "Hide your face well."

Thomas went no further than the town gates.

They were close enough to see the expression of surprise on his face as the guard shrugged and pointed upward. They were close enough to see the discreet transfer of a gold coin from Thomas' hand to the guard's. They were close enough to hear Thomas' instructions to a boy standing just inside the town walls.

He left the boy holding the horse's reins and guarding it just inside the town gate. Thomas then spun on his heels, and half sprinted back to the guard beneath the arch of the town wall.

The guard nodded upon his approach, brought Thomas to the side of the arch, and led him through a door.

"Can it be?" the old man said in hushed tones from their viewpoint in the shadows at the side of the cook shop. Then conviction entered his voice. "It must. Why did I not realize it before?"

"Yes?"

He pointed upward. "The Earl of York is held there." He pointed upward. "Not in the sheriff's prison. I too should have asked the same question he did upon entering York."

Katherine caught the trace of self-doubt. "No," she said as she patted his arm, "we did not want to draw attention to ourselves."

The old man sighed. "Of course."

His sadness disturbs me, Katherine thought as they resumed their watch in silence. *He has never allowed me to see it before.*

Following that sigh, none of her former distractions seemed enjoyable, and the waiting and watching passed very slowly.

Three quarters of an hour later, Thomas stepped outside again, nodded at the guard and marched back to his horse. He took the reins from the small boy, and without looking back, led the horse into the center of York.

Even before Thomas was lost to sight in the swirling crowds, the old man pressed two coins into Katherine's hand.

"One to bribe the same guard he did," he explained. "The other to bribe the guard above."

He spoke with renewed vigor. *An effort to restore her confidence?*

She, of course, did not comment but merely waited for more instructions.

"Reach the earl," he said next. "We must hear what Thomas plans."

"If the earl does not speak?" Katherine asked.

"Tell him it is the only way for him to remove the curse from his family."

Katherine paused. "I do not understand."

"He will," came the reply. "All too well."

Damp stone steps led upward in a dim tight spiral. The guard's leering cackle still echoed in Katherine's mind as she began to climb. *'Tis money poorly spent for an audience, my sweet duckling,* he had said. *The Earl's as powerless as a newborn babe.*

Knowledge is power, Katherine told herself firmly, and if the earl shares his, it will be worth every farthing.

She reached the open chamber at the top of the stairs. The ceiling was low, and its only furniture a crude wooden chair for the upper guard as he watched the doors of the four cells which opened into the chamber.

As she arrived, the guard was unlocking one of the doors.

It startled Katherine. *How does he know I wish to visit the earl? I have not yet placed a bribe in his hand, nor stated my request.*

Her silent question was answered within moments as she saw a prisoner step through the low opened doorway. That prisoner was not the Earl of York.

"You've done well," the prisoner said to the guard. "It is no surprise that Thomas—"

He stopped suddenly as he noticed Katherine. The guard turned too, and they both stared at their quiet visitor.

Black eyes studied her sharply. His cheeks were rounded like those of a well-stuffed chipmunk. Ears thick and almost flappy. Half balding forehead, and shaggy hair which fell from the back of his head to well below his shoulders. A thoroughly ugly man.

And she recognized him.

His name was Waleran. He had once shared a dungeon cell in Magnus with Thomas, placed there as a spy to hear every word he spoke. Katherine had been there too, but as a visitor, disguised beneath a covering wrap of bandage around her face.

Katherine bit her tongue to keep from blurting out her surprise at his presence.

Waleran here meant Thomas had already been discovered, within the hour of arriving in York!

If she too were now discovered. . . .

Katherine fumbled for words, wanting to look as flustered as she felt. "I've brought this for the . . . the former earl," she said, extending the wrapped food as proof that the old man had insisted she carry. "To repay a kindness he once did my father."

Would Waleran believe her? Katherine bowed her head in a humbleness which she hoped hid her flush of fear. In the brief pause as she waited, her heart pounded a dozen times.

How can I warn Thomas? If I leave now, they will suspect!

The prisoner finally spoke to the guard. "Help this pretty creature. I need no escort. And time presses me."

It is Waleran who orders the guard!

The guard grunted agreement and began to unlock the adjacent door

Katherine let her pent-up breath escape slowly as the prisoner brushed past her and began to descend the stairs. She willed herself to move forward slowly, despite the sudden extreme urgency

The guard blocked her movement. Her heart leapt into her throat. But then the guard held out a grimy hand, and she understood. She had forgotten the bribe. With concealed relief, she placed a coin into his palm. He bowed a mock bow and made room for her to enter the prison cell.

Before the door had latched firm behind her, she started in a rushed whisper.

"My good lord," she began, "there is —"

The former Earl of York understood why she halted her words. He touched his face lightly with exploring fingertips of his left hand. "The penalty of losing an earldom. It appears much more terrible than it is," he told her. "There are days I do not feel any pain, and without a mirror.   "

The earl shrugged.

This was not the proud warrior who had stood beside Thomas in battle against the northern Scots. This was not the confident man of royalty who had later decreed that Thomas surrender himself and Magnus. Gone was the trimmed red-blond hair that spoke of Vikings among his ancestors. His face was still broad but no longer remarkably smooth. The blue eyes that matched the sky just before dusk were now dimmed. And gone was the posture of a man at ease with himself and the world he commanded

Instead, his face was crisscrossed with half-healed razor cuts, so that it appeared a giant eagle had raked him repeatedly with merciless talons. His right shoulder hung limp at an awkward angle, popped loose from the collarbone. And his feet were still in splints wrapped with bandages gray-red from long-dried blood.

"Please, my dear, smile," he encouraged her "It would be a small gift well received"

Katherine did so, hesitantly

He waved her to speak "You had something to impart, and it

seemed with great speed."

Katherine nodded. She did not yet know if she could trust her voice. She swallowed a few times, then spoke.

"Your visitor, Thomas," she said. "Would you still wish him dead as you did when he reigned in Magnus?"

2 4

The earl leaned forward with a suddenness that made him wince in pain. "You knew the monk's assistant was Thomas of Magnus?"

"Yes, m'lord. And I fear so shall those who now hold York."

"Impossible," the earl said.

Katherine pointed to a vent in the wall. "Impossible that your voices might carry to the prisoner beside you?"

"Hardly," the earl snorted. "My conversations with him have kept me from losing all sanity here. Yet, even if he eavesdropped, there is nothing he can do."

"Unless he were a spy named Waleran." Katherine explained those days with Thomas in the dungeon beneath Magnus.

The earl clenched his fists. "The prisoner across the wall was one of them? A Druid?"

Katherine replied softly. "Then I need not explain the Druid circle of conspiracy?"

The earl shook his head. "No. Nor the darkness they have placed upon my family for generations. You know of the Druids too? What madness is this?"

Katherine nodded at his first question, and shrugged at his second. She wanted to ask the questions, instead, to learn what Thomas intended, but she dared not press the earl too quickly.

He shuddered. "Druids. We have always been at their mercy."

He touched an empty finger. "There was a ring in our family, passed from father to eldest son, the future Earl of York. With it, these instructions: *Acknowledge the power of those behind the symbol or suffer horrible death.* Five generations ago, the Earl of York refused to listen to a messenger—one whose own ring fit into the symbol engraved upon the family ring. Within weeks, worms began to consume his still-living body. No doctor could cure him. Even a witch was summoned. To no avail. They say his deathbed screams echoed throughout the castle for a week. His son—my great-great-grandfather—then became the new Earl of York. When he outgrew his advisers, he took great care in acknowledging the ring which had been passed to him."

This is the family curse the old man meant!

The earl focused his eyes on the floor. "It only meant responding to a favor asked. A command given. Rarely more than one in an earl's lifetime. Sometimes none. My great-grandfather did not receive a single request. Twenty years ago my father . . . my father stood aside while Magnus fell, despite allegiance and protection promised, he let the new conquerors reign."

He stopped suddenly and darted a sharp look at Katherine. "This is strange, your sudden appearance. You are not one of them?"

She shook her head. "The Druids have already imprisoned you."

The earl gaped in sudden comprehension. "These Priests of the Holy Grail are . . . are . . . "

"And Thomas, I pray, is not," Katherine replied. "Yet you

swore his death. Until today."

"I swore his death because the Druids had forced it upon me, had threatened my sons would die the horrible death of worms. And now you tell me they pose as these priests who now rule my kingdom."

The earl shook his head weakly. "First Thomas with his rash promises. And now you. I feel so old."

Time. Too little time remained. Those heads on spikes were a reminder of the price of failure.

"Rash promise?"

"He offered my kingdom back," the earl said.

"What did Thomas ask of you in return?" Katherine asked quickly. "How will he attempt this? Where goes he next?"

The earl stared strangely at Katherine. "It dawns upon me that you are privy to much, yet are a stranger. Why should you have more of my trust? Why should I believe the story of a spy in the opposite cell? Perhaps you are here to prevent Thomas from succeeding. After all, only a Druid could know what you do."

The earl gained more strength as his thoughts became more certain. "Only a Druid watcher placed at the gates would have known of Thomas' arrival so soon."

Time. Too little time remained. Yet could Katherine betray a secret which had been kept from outsiders for centuries?

She thought of Thomas, of the heads outside this very prison. *Even now as she spoke in this prison cell, did Thomas walk unknowingly to his doom?* Katherine made her decision.

"Few know of the Druids and the evil they pursue," she whispered. "None know there are those who seek to counter them."

The earl's eyes widened. "Another circle?"

Anguish ripped through Katherine for even hinting at that. Since birth, she had been trained to keep what secrets she knew, and had only been permitted to grasp the edges of the truth. It was a secret so precious that not even she knew much more than the existence of the Merlins, only that she was one of them.

The earl repeated himself, almost impatiently. "Another circle?"

How could she bring herself to go beyond that hint and betray even more? But there was Thomas. If he were not a Druid—but as she hoped, one like her—mere observation was no longer enough. Thomas now needed help.

Finally, Katherine forced herself to nod. "Another circle."

Those words hung while she waited until she could remain silent no longer. "Please, Thomas is in danger."

The earl too made his decision based on the pain in Katherine's eyes.

"I gave Thomas my ring," he said, unconciously twisting his now empty finger. "He was to offer it at the castle keep as a method to gain an immediate audience with the man who now holds York for the priests. The new Earl of York."

"That is insane," Katherine blurted. "For what reason would he seek audience with the enemy?"

The earl's reply stunned her.

"Thomas believes he will be able to escape York with a ransom hostage."

2 5

The sunlight blinded Katherine after the dimness of the prison, and she almost stumbled in her rush to rejoin the old man.

For a moment, she felt panic. Her eyes had adjusted, yet she could not see him in the crowd. Then the familiar black cape appeared as he stepped from a nearby doorway.

His face, always difficult to read, was no different as he approached. Yet Katherine knew he was troubled. Instead of waiting for her information with calmly folded arms, he was reaching out to grasp her shoulders and search her face.

"It is not good," Katherine answered his questioning eyes. "Thomas, it seems, seeks his own death."

She explained quickly.

Later, she would tell the old man what she had had to reveal to the Earl of York to get her news.

"We have little choice but to follow, watch, and pray," the old man said. "Too much happens too soon."

He did not elaborate, but turned to march down the street which led to the castle of York.

Katherine remained close behind. Although she did not cast a final look backward, she could not escape the feeling that her every step was watched by those sightless eyes of the heads of the men who had dared rebel against the Priests of the Holy Grail.

They reached the outer courtyard of the castle burdened with a sack of flour that the old man had hurriedly purchased as they had passed by market stalls.

Wolfhounds lazed in the dirt. Servants scurried determined paths through the steady flow of noblemen and ladies who paraded in and out of the entrance with the assured arrogance that money and title provide. Squires stood in conversation with knights casually alert and leaning against stone benches. Other, more humbly dressed squires, held the reins of the horses of their masters.

Of Thomas, or of Waleran, there was no sign. Within seconds, however, Katherine noticed Thomas' now familiar stallion tethered to the trunk of a sapling which struggled for growth in the shadows of the far corner of the court. Tending the horse was the same boy Thomas had hired near the town gate.

She tugged on the old man's arm and whispered, "Thomas is already inside. Do we follow there?"

He shook his head no, and kept his voice low. "If he succeeds, he must come this way. If not, we will bribe servants to tell us the story of his failure and make our plans in accordance."

"How can he hope to succeed?" Katherine asked.

"That too is my question," the old man said softly. He motioned with his head for Katherine to stay at his side, and walked to the boy who tended Thomas' horse.

"The monk's assistant," the old man said to the boy. "Has he promised to return soon?"

"He made a jest," the boy replied. "He said soon, or not at all."

Katherine shivered. It seemed so futile, this direct attack of a single person. *What could Thomas accomplish without an army?*

"We have business to complete," the old man continued as he pointed at the sack of flour that Katherine held. "Yet if he trusted you with his horse, he most surely will trust you with his purchase that we now deliver."

The boy shrugged.

"Find an empty saddle bag," the old man instructed Katherine. "We shall leave it there as he requested."

Katherine complied, as puzzled now as when the old man had bought the flour. When she finished, the old man moved beside her to inspect.

"Keep the boy's attention," he said quietly into her ear.

That task was easy.

Katherine's beauty was uncommon—and apparent even in her modest clothing and beneath a bonnet which placed much of her face in shade. A slight smile was enough to encourage the boy's full stare, and Katherine had no need to further distract him with conversation.

Less than a minute later, the old man rejoined her and they strolled to another portion of the court. Little attention fell upon them. The noblemen and ladies—as Katherine noted—were much too full of themselves and their gossip to look beyond at mere townspeople.

"All that remains is the wait," the old man said. "And the longer it takes, the less his chances."

Katherine closed her eyes and summoned the vision of her last meeting with Thomas.

"How is it then you know what the Druids do?" he had asked. *"If you are not Druids, who are you?"*

That was the question she had wanted to answer more badly than to do anything else in her life. But she could not.

Tears had streamed shiny down her cheeks as she shook her head again.

"I am sorry, m'lady," Thomas had said before banishing her. He had lifted her hand from his arm, then took some of her hair and wiped her face of tears. "I cannot trust you. This battle—whatever it might be—I fight alone."

Those were the words which echoed now. *I fight alone.*

2 6

The old man's voice interrupted her thoughts. "He leaves the entrance now."

Katherine opened her eyes wide. And drew her breath in sharply.

For at Thomas side was another, a person she recognized instantly.

Long slim body, long dark hair, haunting half smile of arrogance, now touched with fear. Isabelle Mewburn. The daughter of the former Lord of Magnus. Isabelle Mewburn. Who had once proclaimed love for Thomas as a means to assassinate him. Isabelle Mewburn. Once held prisoner by Thomas himself.

Katherine could not help but feel a stab of jealousy. She knew that Thomas had once been captivated by that royal grace and stunning features of a finely pale face. And now, clothed in a dress which made the ladies around her look like shabby peasants, Isabelle seemed more heart-winning than ever.

To a casual observer, it might appear that Isabelle merely accompanied the lowly monk's assistant. Yet, as Thomas descended the steps at Isabelle's side, Katherine could see strain etched across her face, and the falseness of the smiles she offered passersby. For Thomas discreetly held her elbow with his left hand. His right hand was hidden beneath his cape.

Katherine guessed he held a dagger, and that he had threatened her life at the slightest attempt of escape, the slightest attempt of obstruction by any of the castle guards. Yet with her dead, Thomas would surely be killed as well.

He was that desperate, that ready to gamble his life.

They reached the courtyard ground.

At the top of the stairs appeared two guards, watching closely every move that Thomas made, and following them both from 10 yards behind.

Thomas guided Isabelle to his horse. The boy removed the reins from the tree and placed them across the horse's neck.

Isabelle balked as Thomas gestured upward, then slumped as he said something Katherine was unable to hear. *A renewed threat to plunge the dagger deep?*

She swung up onto the horse

At that, the idle chatter in the courtyard stopped as if cut by the knife Thomas most certainly held

How strange, how crude, the whispers began, *a royal lady mounting a horse in full dress.*

Some pointed, and all continued to stare.

Isabelle remained slumped in defeat Until Thomas moved to climb up behind her. At the moment his grip shifted on the unseen dagger, she kicked the horse into sudden motion.

Thomas slipped, then clutched at the saddle

His dagger fell earthward.

The next moments became a jumble. Thomas strained to pull himself onto the now galloping horse Isabelle kicked at his face and both nearly toppled from the horse People threw themselves in all directions to avoid the thundering hooves

And the following guards noticed the dagger lying in the dust.

Free now to act, the first one shouted. "Stop him. He kidnaps the lord's daughter!"

Knights scrambled to their horses. Screaming and shouting added to the general panic.

Thomas now had his arms around Isabelle's waist. The horse was galloping in frenzied circles, once passing so close to Katherine that a kicked pebble struck her cheek.

It was his only saving grace, the speed of the horse. Had its panic not been so murderous, Isabelle could have thrown herself free of the horse, and of Thomas. Instead, she could now only cling to the horse's neck.

Thomas finally reached a sitting position in the saddle and roared rage as he reached for the flapping reins. His hands found one, then the other.

"Drop the drawbridge!" the other guard shouted. "Call ahead and tell them to drop the drawbridge."

Thomas pulled the reins. The horse responded instantly to the bit. Thomas spun the horse in the direction of the courtyard entrance, then spurred it forward amid the shouting and confusion.

People once again scattered, except for a solitary knight with a two-handed grip on a long broadsword. The knight braced to swing as the horse approached him.

That iron will cleave a leg!

Katherine wanted to scream.

As the horse reached, then began to pass the knight, arrows flew. Three above Thomas and into the stone wall of the courtyard. The last struck the knight's right shoulder and he dropped in agony. The sword clattered, useless.

Thomas swept through the gateway and thundered toward the drawbridge.

Katherine scrambled with all the other people in the court-yard to catch a glimpse of what might happen next.

Thomas and the horse passed into the shadows of the gateway.

Already, the bridge was a third of the way raised!

Yet Thomas did not slow the horse. A clatter of hooves on stone, then on wood. Then silence as the horse leapt skyward from the rising bridge.

In the hush of disbelief that followed, that sudden silence became a sigh.

Almost immediately, the thundering of more hooves broke that sigh of silence.

Four knights had finally readied their horses and the first charged through the courtyard gate toward the drawbridge.

After seeing Thomas escape, Katherine had relaxed. Now, with a deadly group of four in pursuit, Katherine clenched her fists again and for the first time felt the pain. In her fear, she had driven two fingernails through the skin of her palm and in the heat of action, she had not noticed.

She forced her hands to open again, and ignored the tiny rivulets of blood, but Katherine could not stop the urge to draw huge lungfuls of air, as if she, not Thomas, was in full flight.

Thomas must escape. Yet we are so helpless.

She spun sideways in shock to hear the old man softly laughing.

"Look," he pointed from their vantage point at the front of the gathered crowd. "The drawbridge."

All four horses skidded and skittered to a complete stop in the archway at the drawbridge. One bucked and pawed the air in fear.

For the huge wooden structure was still rising!

Loud bellows of enraged knights broke the air.

"Fools! Winch it down!"

The old man's delighted chuckle deepened. "Such a bridge weighs far too much to be dropped. They'll have to lower it as slowly as it rose. With three roads to choose on the other side, and open fields in all directions, Thomas will have made good his escape!"

They watched until five minutes later, when the drawbridge was finally in place again, they saw the obvious confusion of the knights as they waltzed in hesitant circles at the crossroad beyond the moat.

The old man touched her arm.

"Much has yet to be done," he said. "But if he truly is one of us, we could not ask for more."

Katherine tried to smile.

Yes, she could exult that Thomas still lived. And still lived in freedom.

But he was not alone. And Katherine was not the one at his side.

THE WINDS OF LIGHT CONTINUES ...

In *The Forsaken Crusade,* not even the special knowledge Thomas has gained from his secret treasure of books will prevent the destruction of Magnus. England no longer remains safe for him, and the only solution he finds is to retrace the steps of the Last Crusaders—with a beautiful stranger who trusts him as little as he trusts her. In an Age of Darkness, Thomas must pray the answer he seeks in Jerusalem will be the light he needs to reconquer his kingdom.

HISTORICAL NOTES

Readers may find it of interest that in the times in which the Winds of Light series is set, children were considered adults much earlier than now. By church law, for example, a bride had to be at least 12, a bridegroom 14. (This suggests that upon occasion, marriage occurred at an even earlier age!)

It is not so unusual then, to think of Thomas of Magnus becoming accepted as a leader by the age of 15; many would already consider him a man simply because of his age. Moreover, other "men" also became leaders at remarkably young ages during those times. King Richard II, for example, was only 14 years old when he rode out to face the leaders of the Peasant's Revolt in 1381.

Chapter Three

During medieval times, two main meals were served in the castle keep. Dinner was at 10 or 11 A.M., and supper was at 5 P.M. Forks had not been invented yet. Plates were not common; instead, thick slabs of bread called "trenchers" were generally supplied to hold the day's food.

Monks generally belonged to one of two orders, Franciscan or Cistercian.

Chapter Six
In the early part of King Henry II's reign, a certain clergyman of Bedford slew a knight. Despite overwhelming evidence, he was found innocent in the **bishop's** court, and had the gall to then insult a **royal** judge sent to investigate the matter.

Chapter Nine
It is difficult for historians to agree precisely on the historical King Arthur—while most scholars now regard Arthur's reality as probable, some wonder if he indeed existed at all—but it is commonly held that he was born around A.D. 480.

Some argue that the castle of Camelot existed at Cadbury in southern England, while others choose nearby Glastonbury. Historians do agree, however, that the legends about King Arthur (known as the Arthurian Romances) were finally put to paper by various poets in the 12th and 13th centuries, some seven centuries after the Round Table.

Most of what the old woman relates about the Holy Grail is part of the legend which historians today know circulated from the 12th century on as part of the Arthurian Romances.

As the old woman tells Thomas, the **Holy Grail** is thought to be the cup used by Christ in the Last Supper. *Yet it must be emphasized that the Holy Grail is legend, not biblical truth.* There is no single, clearly defined image of the Grail, nor evidence it ever existed. In fact, even its outward shape is debated. Is it a cup? A shallow dish? A stone? A jewel? Despite, or because of, the lack of historical truth surrounding the Holy Grail, its legend—as Thomas discovers—held much sway over the ignorant peasants of his time, much to the dissatisfaction of the church.

A discerning reader might express amazement that—in an age in which the bulk of people were illiterate—an old beggar woman might know so much about the Holy Grail.

This is not surprising, however. The legend of the Holy Grail was a well-established oral myth, and stories were commonly passed this way from generation to generation.

Indeed, the woman's surprise at Thomas' pretended lack of knowledge is more appropriate, but Thomas, of course, wanted to discover how much influence the false priests might have among his people.

(In other versions of the legend, Joseph of Arimathaea does not go any farther than Europe, and the cup instead is passed on to a man named Bron, who becomes known as the Rich Fisher. [It was told that he received this name because—much as Jesus did—Bron feeds many from the Grail with a single fish.] Bron and his company then settle at Avaron, whom many identify with Avalon/Glastonbury.)

Chapter Twelve

Constructed of stone, Norman (the conquering French) churches were often built upon the ruins of the earlier and wooden Anglo-Saxon churches. Early churches generally consisted of the **nave** where people stood for the services, and a small chancel at the east end of the church for the altar and priest. As time passed, towers, aisles, priest's rooms, and chapels were often added. Thus, the quieter eastern end of the church building of Magnus held the original altar.

Chapter Nineteen

Katherine was correct to express surprise at the existence of books so far from the libraries of kings or of rich monastaries. Books could only be duplicated through laborious hand copying. Books were so rare and valuable that some historians estimated that before Gutenberg invented the press in the early 1400s, the number of books in all of Europe only numbered in the thousands—fewer than the number found today in a single standard elementary school!

Chapter Twenty-One

Even today, the religous miracle of **unclotting blood** is hailed each year in Naples, Italy, as it has been for more than six hundred years. Believers there say a sealed sample of the clotted blood of Saint Januarius (martyred in the year A.D. 305) has turned into liquid each year since 1389, and the event now draws crowds of thousands, and a television audience numbering in the millions.

Scientists, however, claim this jam-like gel may simply consist of a mixture of chalk and hydrated iron choride lightly sprinkled with salt, a substance they say could have easily been produced by medievel alchemists.

As for the **Weeping Statue**, it may be probable that the effects of condensation brought on by quick changes from heat to cold were little understood by the illiterate masses of peasants.

Chapter Twenty-Two

Modern-day **York**, in the the North York Moors, is a substantial city, but its inner core is still marked by the thick walls of ancient York, walls which still bear some of the chambers mentioned in this chapter.

Beheading traitors and leaving their heads for all to see was common, and unfortunately, one of the more merciful ways of dealing with rebels.